Beth and the Mistaken Identity

Alicia Cameron

Dedication:

To Rebecca, for her help and enthusiasm

© Alicia Cameron 2019. The author's moral rights have been asserted. This is a work of fiction. Any resemblance to person or persons living or dead is coincidental.

Chapter 1

As Beth clutched her carpetbag in the inn taproom, she waited patiently to be noticed, terrified and defiant at once. If she dropped her chin now it would be the end of her. There were a few working men standing at the board where the ale was distributed, a few gentlemen drinking around tables and a buxom lass of about sixteen serving the gentlemen. Beth was reassured that there were so many persons of elegance. A table by a mullioned window seated two gentlemen of the most superior attire, with a driving coat of many capes cast over a chair, not yet hung on the pegs allotted for same by the door. Beth had a ridiculous desire to put this right. This inn was used frequently by the *ton*, as well as by professional gentlemen, and she had chosen it carefully. She put her chin a little higher in the air as she waited to be attended to.

A gentleman from the window table attempted to put his arms around the red-haired serving wench, and she neatly dodged him, but did not succeed in avoiding the pinch he aimed at her behind. Facing her, Beth saw the girl's face blush, but to her surprise the serving girl giggled towards the gentleman, but removed herself further from his orbit, losing the smile as she turned away. Beth's eyes opened wide. Was this the fate that awaited her, too? She had visited this respectable inn twice before, but *then* she had her duties to attend to, or was with Miss Sophy, and no such behaviour came within her orbit. But now ... The world away from Foster Hall was a terrible place.

His companion, the elder and more handsome of the two had not witnessed this, he having strode over to the fire to warm himself, gazed into the depths thoughtfully. He turned, and she met a pair of sapphire blue eyes. In shock, she could not look away soon enough, but after three long seconds managed to drop her eyes to the floor. 'Desist, you termagant, there is a lady present,' she heard the gentleman say to his companion. He had, somehow, noticed then.

The blond-haired gentleman, a little younger, looked over his shoulder and said in a drunken drawl. 'Beg your pardon, dreadful behaviour, I'm sure-'

'Yes, that is quite enough!' said the other tersely.

She nodded, blushing, and realised that her simple but stylish dress and pelisse, only two seasons old, had given the gentleman quite the wrong impression. An impression of the kind that had already had her pitched her out of her respectable life and into this terrifying other existence, whose pitfalls loomed large. *How did I get here?* she asked herself again. But she knew how. Miss Sophy. Obeying, or not obeying, Miss Sophy was bound to lead to this end.

She looked back towards the board, where three leering grooms were adding to her new vision of hell, and was glad when a bustling figure of a round man, with thinning red hair about a genial face, came out. He plastered a smile of welcome on his face as he saw her, and said, 'How can I help you, miss? I'm afraid we have but one chamber left — I could have a truckle bed set up for your maid.'

'My — maid?' How on earth was she to tell him now that she had come to ask for work? Especially after she had seen the treatment meted out to his serving girl, who from her round face and red hair had to be his *daughter*. Her misery made her do the Second Most Stupid Thing in her life. 'My maid fell ill and I had to leave her behind at the last stage, I'm afraid.'

'Well,' said the landlord with a slight change of tone. 'I'm not sure we can accommodate you—'

'Nonsense, my dear Stopes, the young lady must be accommodated,' said a suave voice.

The landlord bowed lowly, 'Very good, my lord. Would you wish any refreshment to be brought to your chamber, miss? A little supper perhaps?'

Beth was starving, but this was not the best use of the coin in her purse. 'That is not necessary, thank you.' She turned with Miss Sophy's demeanour, if a little more stiffly, to the owner of the sapphire blue eyes. 'I thank you, my lord, for your intervention, and now I must retire.'

The landlord looked not at her, but at her aristocratic companion, who wore a buff cutaway long tailed coat over a high necked waistcoat. His eyes, set in a handsome face with a deeply cleft chin, looked at her kindly. 'Take a seat with me here.' He indicated a settle by the taproom fire, removed from the gentlemen he had been seated with. It looked inviting, and it was public after all, but Beth stiffened even more. 'Bring the young lady some tea and cake, Stopes, and perhaps some chicken?'

Everything today had gone wrong, and this was the first kindness shown to her for a long time. Beth considered that eating on the gentleman's shilling seemed sensible, as she was now to pay for a room because she was too proud and afraid to do other. So she sat, still stiff, waiting while he joined her at the opposite end, a respectable distance between them. 'So, should we begin with the maid? There is no maid, is there?' Beth's eyes flew to his in terror. His eyes were gentle. 'What is it? Have you run away from school?'

Beth was nineteen now, seven years into her erstwhile orderly career, but she knew she looked sixteen. 'Yes — no — sir — I mean my lord.'

'My name is Tobias Brunswick, Marquis of Wrexham. May I have the privilege of knowing yours?'

'I — I —' Beth stalled. Her copy of Miss Sophy's accent, if not in her superior tones, was holding, but she sounded much more hesitant, more like the fifteen-year-old schoolgirl he thought her. He was a marquis. Even in Foster Hall or in London, Beth had never met such lofty a personage. Yet those eyes were true, and somehow reminded her of her brother, Jem.

'You need not tell me if you do not wish to. But I *would* like to help. Funds running a little low?' Beth stiffened once more, not meeting his eyes. 'Oh don't pucker up, my lady, I don't wish to pry. But if you are returning to London, I could help you.' He laughed as she clutched her hands together more firmly and looked away. 'That did sound ominous! I should tell you that I am awaiting my sister here and we shall all be travelling on to London tomorrow. So you shall be royally chaperoned. My sister is a *princess*, you see!'

He's making fun of her, she was sure now, and she resolved to leave, but at this moment some victuals arrived on a table before her. Nothing much could happen in a public taproom, she supposed, though she looked to the neighbouring table and saw that the serving girl was once more attending to the rowdy young gentlemen. With a swift look to them, the man he had called 'termagant' said something in a low tone to the young redhead and her smile froze. She widened it however, and left, the smile dropping like a hot coal as she turned away. Beth's eyes met the girl's and as hers tried to convey her pity, the girl blushed her thanks.

'I did not know that a girl in a respectable inn could be so treated,' she said, with hardly a thought, but still in Miss Sophy's accents.

'Oh, Stopes, you mean? He has his eye on the proprieties. He would have given you the chamber eventually, I'm sure.'

'No. Your friend.'

'Did he talk to you? I didn't think — oh you mean to the *servant*? It is kind of you to notice her.'

Her eyes flashed fury at him before she could help herself. Of course, a servant was not a *person*, most especially, she thought, to a marquis. She dropped them quickly. She trembled. What was she thinking, showing her thoughts? Yet another Very Stupid Thing. Her absolute terror of her fate was making her unbalanced and all the discipline she had learnt was crashing around her.

She looked up fearfully. The gentleman had raised his eyebrows. But he did not look angry, on the contrary he looked even more kindly. 'You have suffered such treatment yourself. Was it at school — did you run away because some blackguard offered you an insult? Never mind, you may be quite comfortable now.'

Beth thought about her little attic bedroom, with the ample blankets and sometimes even a hot brick, if Nancy had a minute, that she would never see more. Would she be so safe again? She shook herself and began to eat the food provided. As the marquis had ordered it, extra care had been taken, and she set upon it as elegantly as she could. She was hungry, yes, but she was also aware of the need to stuff herself against future lack. She remembered hunger very well.

His Lordship's attention was diverted by a shout in the yard. A coach was pulling up and a great many people seemed to attend it. The Marquis raised an eyebrow and smiled at her. 'My sister, I believe. She never arrives quietly. He got up from the table and bowed as a cry of 'Wrexham! Where are you, can you see to everything? Trixie has been most fearfully sick on my pelisse.'

As the gentleman attended the vision in a bronze French pelisse with a fur stole slipping from her shoulders and the highest poke bonnet Beth had ever seen, the young girl slid her gaze round the room and stuffed her bag with two apples, and wrapped three small cakes in a napkin before adding them. The red haired girl emerged from the kitchen before she had finished and caught her, a slight crease at her brow. Beth looked piteously at her and she smiled.

My dearest Lady Ernestine, (the missive read),

I have written to you with an express purpose, though I must first of all say that I hope that you are all well at Horescombe House and that the weather is seasonable with you and with your esteemed and venerable grandfather whose noble character and un-

remitting kindness to me, a distant family member on his mother's side only, and that a family perfectly respectable in our own county, but normally far beneath the notice of such a distinguished peer of the realm, whose own family has been in England since the Conqueror no doubt, and who had no need to notice my second cousin Albertina, except for his kindness and her own beauty. Please give him my every sincere expression of respect and also affection, if he did not find the latter presumptuous, which is a fault that Florencia says I must seek to quell in myself. 'Pride cometh before a fall' and heavens knows I should not like to give way to pride so I pray you will withhold any expression of affection, which I do of course hold for your grandfather, that noble lord, who is never far from all our thoughts and prayers, I assure you, especially on market day when his beneficence adds once more to our comfort and good health. It seems such a short time ago when he came riding to meet us, though it was a full twenty miles from London, coming to claim our dear Albertina as his betrothed. He was such a handsome young man, with flowing golden locks, and is still as handsome I am sure, though I have heard that his hair has left him like that of many blond men, and he is restricted to the house with gout which is something that Papa suffered from, too, and whilst it is such a dispiriting malady for the sufferer, Florencia holds that it is also painful for those who live among them, for there is no use in saying that Papa had an equable temper, for he had not. This is not to say that His Lordship will behave in any way less than his no-

bility demands, whatever the circumstances, even if it is a dreadfully painful condition which would drive a less elevated mind quite mad.

This may be a little tied up, but I hope you will say all that is proper to your grandfather and not repeat any of my absurdities, which I beg of your generous spirit to ignore or pardon, whichever is the most appropriate. And you too, my dear, I beg your pardon, I'm being presumptuous again, pray take my sister's, and my very best sentiments and gratitude for all your endeavours on our behalf, which I assure you are not forgotten and most earnestly appreciated. Florencia is calling for dinner and as you can judge the matter is urgent, though I know that for you it is not probably as urgent as it is for me who is not in the thrust of London performing the important duties, and social engagements that you do which I can have no notion of, never having visited the metropolis in my life, Florencia saying that I was extremely selfish to wish to do so when young, as it burdened my dear Papa with guilt that he was unable to take me even to see the Wild Beasts in the Exchange for a day, so I have of course quelled this insensitivity on my part and I hope that poor Papa did not hold that dream of mine against me before he died, thirty years later.

I shall leave you to judge whether there is anything to be done about this situation which I hardly liked to mention to you were it not for your unlooked for attention to me and my sister in writing every month, and I promise that I will only mention the subject this once, which Florencia has insisted on most forcefully, and I agreed of course. As you can imagine to such a temperament as Florencia's, it is almost unbearable to ask anyone for support and I assure you that we would not, except that we are in need of another opinion, a more worldly view, which if your youth precludes you from providing perhaps you might ask some other, mentioning no names, of course, and not at all wishing to be presumptuous. I must hasten to finish this or it will not catch the mail coach and it would not do to miss it, as I did with the order for faux silk stockings which unpardonable delay caused Florencia to have to attend church with a darned toe which was not at all visible but which chafed her sorely I assure you.

I remain your most affectionate and respectful cousin,

Wilhelmina Fosdyke.

Lady Ernestine Horescombe, in a striped day dress of a most fashionable cut, some black curls escaping beneath a complexly wrapped bandeau of the same fabric, read the letter again, 'Of all the absurdities! Miss Fosdyke has written-'

'Which one?' said a tall, elegant old gentleman, with hair loss as described in the letter, but showing no trace of gout-induced bad humour today, thankfully.

'The youngest, Grandpapa.'

'Thank the lord. The other terrifies me, even from a distance,' he mumbled into his journal.

'She writes to ask my advice, she sounds worried—'

'What concerns her?'

'That is the absurdity, she does not say. I wonder—' Lady Ernestine stopped. She looked at her grandfather, who looked up at her with enlightenment dawning.

'Sophy!' they both said at once.

'Good heavens — what has she done now?'

Lord Wrexham's sister greeted Beth with an outstretched hand. She was tall, even without the help of the poke bonnet, and slender as a reed. 'Now *where* do I know you from?'

Beth could feel her eyes widen, as she tried without success to wonder if she had ever sewn on a lace trim or retied an errant ribbon for this young lady at some house party in Foster Hall or London, but she did not think she could have forgotten this vision of elegance. She managed a faint, 'I do not think we have met—'

'We *have* and *recently!*' pursued that young lady.

'You remind me that I have not the privilege of knowing your name,' said the marquis, when Beth hesitated to answer. 'You must know,' he said pleasantly to his sister, 'that our young friend is rather shy and I believe she may have run away from school and does not trust us with her name.'

'I beg pardon, my lord,' said Beth rather desperately, 'My name is Elizabeth - Elizabeth-' she looked around for inspiration and saw the Fox and

Hound Inn sign through the window, 'Fox.'

'No,' said Wrexham's sister, handing a pug dog to him and removing her bonnet, *'that's* not it.'

'You must excuse my sister, Miss Fox,' said his lordship, narrowly avoiding the sharp teeth of the pug, 'she has no manners at all. Royalty, you know. Miss Fox, may I present my sister Princess Emmeline Herzberg-Wittgenstein.'

Shrugging off her fur and handing it to the young gentleman who'd accompanied Wrexham, who took it with a bow, 'Princess!'

As Beth widened her eyes, the green eyed beauty, now displaying her rich brown hair tied in a complex coiffure, said, 'Oh, ignore the title, it amuses my brother. My late husband was prince of the tiniest principality in the world, which I left as soon as ever I could, I assure you. Thankfully, we had no children to tie me to the dratted place and his brother is now safely installed as ruler, and I need never go there again.'

Beth deepened her curtsy while the young woman looked amused. 'I must marry again, someone untitled I think, so that I may be plain Lady Emmeline once more. I assure you my rank causes hostesses everywhere a problem with precedence. I mean, do they *really* want to upset the Duchess of Devonshire or someone by putting *me* before her?'

Beth thought of Mr Larkins, the butler of Foster Hall, and her late employer being faced with this problem and smiled. 'Oh, yes!' she gasped unintentionally.

The young woman narrowed her fascinating eyes again and said, 'Now, *where* have we met?'

Beth was now quite afraid. *Had* she encountered this lady before? And if the princess remembered, as she seemed determined to do, Lord Wrexham would be angry and have her thrown out of the inn, to walk the country roads in the dark. She shivered at the thought. 'I think I must be more tired than I knew. Thank you for your kindness, my lord, your highness, I must retire to my chamber.'

Bobbing a curtsy to them all, Beth turned. 'Miss Fox! We will meet at breakfast! We leave for London at ten of the clock and there is room in the carriage to spare, for Mr Tennant and I are on horseback.'

Beth, achingly aware of her small resources, thought it insanity to refuse this offer, for with this hope of a position gone, London seemed the next best hope, but the memory of the princess might return. She sufficed by saying, 'You are too kind, my lord.' Which he may take as acquiescence if he wished.

In her room, Beth was tired by her own fear. Not much of this was her fault. She remembered the day, a year ago now, when she had been appointed lady's maid to Miss Sophy. She had been so proud and later, when she got to know her young lady better, had felt so fortunate to have such a beautiful and vivacious mistress who had taken her into her confidence at once, who dispensed clothes and gifts to her maid with great regularity, who was a triumph to dress and coiffure. The full disaster of her appointment did not become apparent until a month or so. For Miss Sophy was a devil.

She had just removed her dress when a knock sounded at the door. She opened it a crack, trembling. Princess Emmeline stood there, her green eyes dancing.

'Your name is *not* Elizabeth Fox!'

Chapter 2

The marquis saw his sister enter the chamber that presumably held the young girl from the taproom, and hoped that Emmeline could get her to confide a little. Emmeline had escaped from the school she had been sent to when she had tortured too many governesses at home, and could certainly understand the behaviour that might have brought the girl here. But the girl with the soft brown hair and sweet face was cut from different cloth than his sister. She was proud, but afraid, and somehow she brought out the protective instinct in Wrexham - a new experience. Emmeline had never needed protection that he could see, she had no nerves at all. He wondered what had brought the child here. She had not quite agreed that she had run from school, but she had blushed when he said it and given herself away. If Emmeline could get her real story they could perhaps help.

Nick Tennant, parting from him at the bedchamber door with a drunken pat on his back, said, 'What shall we do with your little filly when we reach London?' This pulled him up short. Surely the girl was travelling to her family? He hoped so. Drat it, what was he to do with her if Emmeline did not get her story tonight? They could hardly abandon such a sweet young thing on the London streets without any protection. He frowned and ignored Tennant's question. Wait and see what Emmeline could uncover.

'Let me in, won't you?' Beth did as she was asked automatically and her hands dropped to her sides, all resistance gone, awaiting her fate. The princess came in with a swish of silk and if Beth had been herself she could have admired her carriage dress, the same green as her eyes, made high at the neck and tight at the bust and sleeves, with a full skirt at the back allowing for comfort on the journey.

'I didn't meet you, after all,' Beth still held her breath, 'but you were pointed out to me at a masquerade at Vauxhall Gardens.' Beth sank to the bed, feeling the blood leave her face. She wrung her hands together. The princess sat beside her, not seeming to notice her distress, talking as though this whole thing were a joke. 'I asked who the woman in pink was and someone told me. You are not Elizabeth Fox, but Sophy Ludgate!' Beth gasped and then gave a choking laugh. She remembered that night, Miss Sophy had the pink domino and she the green, but her dress (she shook as she remembered how shocking that dress was, only two sheer layers and a décolletage that barely covered her) was pink. Her informant had named Miss Sophy as the lady in pink whereas the princess was referring to the *dress.* 'Where did you get that dress? I really have to know — it was too wonderfully shocking!'

'Madame Godot's,' said Beth automatically, but then gave a nervous laugh. It was too ridiculous. But the release of tension at being able to stay here tonight and even save the stage fare to London was acute. And all because she was believed to be Miss Sophy.

'Your exploits are legendary,' said the princess, 'you tack near to the line, but never seen to go over it.'

Beth sighed, thinking of the times she personally had hauled Miss Sophy back over the line quite literally. She sank onto the bed.

'But you know, my girl, you must be careful.' The princess sat and took Beth's hand. 'Having a free spirit I understand, I had one myself as a girl,' Beth considered that the princess could be no more than twenty-two or twenty-three years, yet she did seem so sophisticated, 'but it can lead one to be irredeemably lost.'

'My name isn't—' Beth did not wish to continue this charade, the princess's kindness, however casual, did not deserve lies.

Beth and the Mistaken Identity

'Now, now!' she said, 'You seem a little frightened. Perhaps you have already sailed too close to the wind? And are escaping home for a while?' The princess got up. 'Well, the journey to London will have you royally chaperoned — it is absurd isn't it? It was only a few years ago that I was considered quite as naughty as you!'

Beth was trembling, the princess must have felt it, for she leaned over and kissed Beth lightly on the cheek, saying, 'Sleep now. You have fallen into good hands, I assure you!'

Beth, left alone, thought about the misery of lying. She was an honest girl, maidservants who were other did not last long in the best houses, but since she had become acquainted with Miss Sophy, she had naturally become inured to falsehoods. She supposed she could endure this falsehood for the length of the trip to London. She knew, since she had been cast off without a character, she could not apply at any great house, or really any respectable house. But perhaps a job at an inn, where the references were not so strictly adhered to, was something she could hope for. Or perhaps a job in a milliner's, sewing in a damp basement and living in some … No. An inn would at least afford her accommodation — though after seeing the treatment that the red-haired waitress was offered, she could not help but shudder. Mrs Shuttleworth, the pious cook at Foster Hall, where she had worked since she was twelve, had often spoken in dreadful accents about losing one's character, about the degradations, fearfully but obscurely referenced, that befell a young girl cast off by the family. Only one day into her fall from grace and Beth was already seeing what might be in store for her.

She slid beneath the covers but a knock at the door was followed by a swift intrusion by a red head, and the maid then slid in.

'Excuse me, Miss, I brought this for you.' She put down a checked cloth beside Beth on the bed and Beth opened it. It contained two more apples and joy of joy, an orange.

They looked at each other.

'Thank you,' said Beth, glad not to be pretending. 'How did you know?'

The girl leaned over and touched the callous on the inside of her forefinger left by repetitive stitching, and another on her thumb. 'My mother had such. She was a seamstress. I needed to explain to you that my da would tan the hide off'n a working man who offered me such insults as you have seen. But with the quality, see, it's best not to upset them. Though allow it to go too far, he will not.' She said this, Beth knew, more in defence of her father than herself. Beth smiled, unable to say anything. The red head disappeared as quickly as she came.

But I do not have a father to protect me.

Something in all this, something in the marquis's kind eyes and protective demeanour, made her know tomorrow was taken care of at least. And somehow, despite her terrors, she slept deeply.

Chapter 3

Lady Ernestine Horescombe read for most of the journey to Foster Hall, choosing not to fear the worst until fully informed. Being something like a guardian to Miss Sophy Ludgate for the last five years, she was naturally far from hope of avoiding disaster, but on the other hand the rules of conduct that the two Misses Fosdyke, mousy Miss Wilhelmina and martinet Miss Florencia, were a great deal stricter than Lady Ernestine had ever thought necessary. Perhaps that was the problem, Ernestine (then but twenty years old herself) had encouraged her Grandpapa to be overly lax with the young girl. But this was a fleeting thought. Sophy was a handful, and had arrived so. She had progressed from swimming in the lake when forbidden to do so at twelve years old, and riding a horse she was similarly forbidden, which Ernestine had found mildly amusing. She was not a tree-climber or a physical risk-taker herself, but she had never seen why a girl being such was less acceptable than a boy. But as Sophy had grown toward womanhood, it was impossible to explain to her why her wilfulness was more dangerous now than it had once been. Perhaps Ernestine's understanding of the earlier adventures had made Sophy worse. But Ernestine could not trouble herself with the whys and wherefores now. She would need her energy to deal with whatever the young girl had done this time.

Sophy had been sent away from London to Foster Hall to be looked after by Lady Foster, after a series of shocking behaviours that would draw censure from the world if they became generally known. There was the time that Sophy had kissed a Lieutenant Prescott, who was enough of a friend to drop a word in Ernestine's ear, disengaging himself and describing it as a young girl's high spirits, but with a warning in his tone — *if it had been a less honourable gentleman* ... And the time that Sophy had escaped the leash and persuaded her friend Miss Lamb to join her on a trip to the theatre, a treat she had been refused because of another incident. The girls went in disguise, even rinsing their hair another colour, but Sophy had the recklessness to wear a particularly charming tiara, belonging to her dead mama, which was famous in its own right. Thankfully, a cousin had been in the foyer there and took the young girls to her box. But, unable to resist Sophy's piteous pleas, had merely banished them to the back, removed the tiara and sent it to the Horescombes via her footman, and afterwards took both girls home safely.

Miss Lamb was not permitted to meet with Sophy again, though her mother had assured Ernestine that the matter would not be referred to by her. And all this and more before her first season. Lady Foster, to whom Sophy was sent, was a recluse and, Grandpapa had assured Ernestine, a disciplinarian. What trouble could Sophy get into in Foster Hall, away from London's bright lights?

Ernestine had visited quite frequently during the year, and Sophy had sat with her remarkably quietly, only begging once each visit for a return to London. And by letter of course. She cited her own good behaviour frequently and Lady Ernestine was considering giving her a season next year, when she might at last be able to comport herself like a lady, and the diversions of the season might curb her seeking adventure. Lady Foster had seemed to be a rather vague and sickly guardian — having the tendency, said Ernestine to her grandpapa, to quack herself, dosing herself with enough *medicaments* to fell a horse, for largely invisible ailments. However, there was a moment on an early visit when Ernestine had been glad to see the iron fist in the velvet glove (as it were).

Sophy had ignored a plaintive request for aid to search for her shawl from Lady Foster, effecting not to hear it. Her ladyship had not asked again. When Ernestine had looked her displeasure, Sophy had offered the aid after all, but was sweetly gestured away. However, when later Ernestine had offered to drive Sophy into the village to visit her friend Miss Jessop, and perhaps the Fosdyke sisters, Lady Foster had denied the possibility in a soft voice. 'I'm afraid I cannot spare dear Sophy this afternoon, Lady Ernestine. My maladies chain me to my couch as you see, and I require my dear girl to write invitations for my card party, and to consult with cook and — oh, all manner of things that I am not yet able to do.'

A mulish look came over Sophy's face at this and she said, with a semblance of politeness. 'Oh, dear Lady Foster, I assure you I can carry out these tasks when I come back from the village.'

'It is like you to overestimate your youthful energy, Sophy, but you know, my sweet that you were laid up only last week with the sick headache.'

Two sets of eyes met, unmasked for a second. Lady Ernestine thought that Lady Foster had her own way to deal with Sophy's starts and she had ridden away rather content. Sophy with a sick headache was highly unlikely, much more might it have been some ploy in the game for dominance that this pallid lady was apparently winning. Grandpapa was rather wiser than Ernestine had given him credit for.

But now...

Larkins' face, as he handed down Lady Ernestine, was of the same impassive complexion as always, befitting a butler. But that he had not allowed the footman to perform this service was enough of a clue to Ernestine that things were grave indeed.

She stopped to remove her old plaid cloak and bonnet, the cloak her grandmama's and the bonnet incongruously smart. 'Something troubles you, Larkins?'

He coughed. 'I am sorry to say that Miss Sophy is without a maid at present. I admit it is a concern to me as a disorder in the running of the house. It will not be easy to replace her with such an accomplished girl from around here. Perhaps you might send a London girl, Lady Ernestine?'

Ernestine had been running her grandfather's home for long enough to understand the subtext. 'Was the girl cast off? How long was she here?'

'Seven years, my lady,' said Larkins gravely.

'Good God!' said Ernestine, falling back on her grandfather's language.

'Indeed, your ladyship!'

'Where is Lady Foster?'

'She is unwell, your ladyship. I believe she may not be able to see you today.'

'And Miss Sophy?'

'Also in her bed. Beginning a chill, I believe.'

'Have the carriage returned. I will visit the village.'

In the comfortable, but tiny, front room of the Misses Fosdyke's cottage, the excessive salutations of Miss Wilhelmina, were roughly ended by Miss Florencia. 'Wil-helm-ina!' She herself curtsied deeply, but gave no further sense of being overwhelmed by the visit. Lady Ernestine rather approved of her.

'What has Sophy done now?' was her direct attack on the elder Miss Fosdyke.

With a look directed at her sister to stay silent, Miss Fosdyke told her, then added. 'A young person, of previously sterling character, has been cast off by this adventure. While she was wrong, no doubt, to have gone along with it, she was only obeying her mistress. Had she come to us, I would have taken her in. Though how I should have paid her it would be hard to tell. We have known her since she was a child, come to Foster Hall as a kitchen maid. She delivered many notes to us from her mistress. She seemed clean in her habits and diligent. Miss Sophy hardly knows what she has done to her.'

This was grave indeed. And the upshot was that Lady Ernestine returned to Foster Hall and walked straight up the stairs to Sophy's bedroom.

Sophy Ludgate was happy to tell Ernestine Horescombe her method when asked. Ernestine felt that the chit was rather proud of herself. She had arranged to dress herself and her maid in dominoes borrowed from her friend Miss Lamb, to whom she had applied by letter. Miss Lamb had forgone the trip to Vauxhall herself, aware that her mama would, she'd said, "have hysterics and very likely expire" if she did such a thing again. However, she engaged to have Sophy met by her maid who would bring the dominoes and masks (which her mother and she acquired for a masked ball that season) to Sophy's carriage.

The escape was easily achieved. She had only to go to bed early that night, get herself and Beth dressed for a ball, minus the dominoes which they would retrieve in London, and escape from the first floor window of an adjoining room which had a strong tree branch adjacent. She'd had to push Beth, who had a silly fear of heights, out of the window enough so that she had no option but to climb on the branch. 'It was so funny to see her feet dangling, frantically kicking for support which was only just below her,' Sophy laughed. 'The very worst thing was that my dress got caught on a branch, and I feared that it would tear and be ruined, but I called for Beth and she climbed up and released it.' Ernestine looked at her slanted eyes, full of confiding candour and laughter, and ground her teeth. 'Then we found the carriage at the gates and drove off.' She held up a little imperious hand and added, 'Do not ask me who supplied it, for I shall never tell. I am not a tattle-tale who repays her friends with betrayal. I am true blue and shall never die!'

'And your maid, Sophy? A girl who worked in this house for seven years, cast off because of your little scheme. Have you not betrayed her?'

'Oh, you have been listening to Miss Fosdyke. She took me aside after church and rang me such a peal, all because of Beth. If Beth had stayed, I'm sure I could have got Lady Foster to change her

Beth and the Mistaken Identity

mind. I *did* say that it was all my idea.'

'No one doubts it was your idea, Sophy, but Lady Foster cannot have a maid who is no longer reliable. And it was you who made her so.'

'She need not have gone with me, after all. I meant it as a treat for her.'

'And now? You realise what dangers there are for a girl with no position?'

'Oh, but Beth will be alright, I assure you. She has very likely got a new position already. She is very clever and resourceful. Look—' she stood and pirouetted in her yellow dress, 'she fashioned this for me, only from an illustration in *La Belle Assemblée*, no pattern at all.'

'But she has *no character* from Lady Foster. Her ladyship said that she could not, in conscience, provide one after your little escapade.'

'Then I expect she has gone to London. She knows the city, you know, for you remember she came with me from Foster Hall last year.' Ernestine strove to remember her: a pretty, quiet young girl, whom she saw as Sophy's shadow, and hardly noticed at all. Sophy said, virtuously, 'I gave her a sovereign, you know, and told her to write to me when she was settled.'

'You are a hideous child, Sophy. I only wish you could walk one week in that poor girl's shoes to know what you have done. You shall now pack up your belongings and come home with me.'

Sophy hugged her. 'To London? Oh, how lovely! Thank you, Lady Ernestine.'

'It is not a reward, Sophy. I expect my grandfather will keep you to the house for a very long time.'

But Sophy was not to be depressed. Already, Ernestine supposed, watching as the young beauty ran about her chamber, she was plotting ways of escape to see the sights and maybe more. But Ernestine's sympathy for the young girl had run out, and she planned a very different kind of visit to London than Sophy had enjoyed last year. Very different.

'Only the essentials, Sophy,' called Lady Ernestine after her, 'the rest can be sent by carrier. We shall be too many in the coach.'

The most wonderful part of Ernestine's day was viewing Sophy Ludgate's face when she entered the carriage and saw that as well as her guardian, the two Misses Fosdyke, in their rusty black bonnets and unfashionable wool cloaks, were already ensconced. Her jaw dropped, and she met her mentor's eye, while Ernestine sat as smug as a cat, raising one eyebrow. Ernestine gave herself to her book then, tuning out any but the first sentence of Miss Wilhelmina's gratitude, the whole of which went on for some miles and was only ended by a nip from Miss Florencia. Unfortunately this brutal reminder served to start a rush of apologies instead. Two miles of this and finally Miss Wilhelmina fell under her sister's eye again and, after removing her prayer book from her reticule, said,

'Ah, I will take a leaf from Lady Ernestine's book and read, I believe.'

There was some respite for perhaps two more miles and Ernestine took the opportunity to glance at Sophy again, having the satisfaction of seeing her look disturbed. Miss Wilhelmina now began on the beauty of the countryside as they passed, quoting poets who described sylvan settings very different to their views from the carriage. This lasted rather longer than her previous perorations, for Miss Florencia had fallen asleep and there was no one to stop her sister's flights of fancy. Ernestine could only wonder how her grandfather would take to his new guests. But he was rather too tied to his library, after all, Ernestine thought ruthlessly. The Misses Fosdykes' presence would be a welcome agent of driving him out of the house and into society once more.

The arrival of the party at Horescombe House was everything that Ernestine's sense of the ridiculous could have hoped for.

'Good God!' said her grandfather and took himself off to another room. He poked his head around the door after he left. 'Erm! Welcome ladies. Ask Socrates if there is anything you desire. I must just... Hrrumph. Sophy. Go to your room!' he ended severely. 'I will talk to you later.' With this he left, having scared even Miss Wilhelmina silent.

Ernestine followed him, saying to Socrates, whose real name was Williams, 'Pray bring refreshments for the ladies, Socrates, and have someone show them to their rooms.'

'Oh, Lady Ernestine—' began Miss Wilhelmina, in grateful accents.

But Ernestine had gone.

Chapter 4

It was unchristian to lie. Beth knew this, and as they sped to London, she was perfectly sure that the lie about her name (which neither the marquis nor his sister the princess believed at any rate) was now being compounded, not by her expanding it, but by her silence. Sins of omission were as bad as sins of commission. She tried to think what she would do when she reached the capital and found that her head froze at every plan she made. There were jobs at inns which now, after seeing the fate of the landlord's daughter, seemed tainted by the prospect of unwanted attentions from men. Respectability was such a fragile thing, she was discovering. Possibly in the case of the landlord's daughter these daily insults from gentlemen did not lead much further, but for a girl on her own with no family protection, she was afraid of how much more pressing the gentlemen could be. She supposed even the men who *worked* at the inn could pose a problem. In a gentleman's house, with a butler keeping a close eye on staff behaviour, a young girl could be almost free of assault. But in a public inn? Was it too much to expect to be able to live a respectable life?

Beth forgave herself for her lie, because she was thus trying both to survive and to save her virtue. Perhaps she had been too long with Miss Sophy — whose ability to lie to get exactly what she wanted was prodigious. What would she do if she was Miss Sophy in this situation? What did she want? To enter a gentleman's house as a maidservant and perhaps one day reach the heady heights of housekeeper? To go back home where she was safe and appreciated? But it was not to be.

The marquis had handed first his sister, and then herself into the carriage, retaining her hand for a moment before saying, 'You really must not be afraid, my child. You tremble still.'

It had been Beth's experience that gentlemen of rank did not live up to the picture of grandeur that their titles suggested. Lord Thornton had been but five feet tall. Sir Reginald Pine had been extremely portly with an eye-twitch, while Lord Staines, while handsome, had seemed to Beth so unbearably smug that it made her think of Peters, the under-butler at Foster Hall, who considered himself above them all, and was frequently made to look a fool by Larkins the butler. The Marquis of Wrexham however had a very tall, athletic frame, exquisite taste in tailoring, and yet a face that was not precisely the handsome of the classical figures in portraits, being scored with harsh lines down his cheeks. But it was more pleasing to most women, Beth thought, than the bland handsomeness of the loathsome Mr Tennant, who looked as callow as his behaviour. It was the face of a man of force and reason, someone to rely on. His sapphire eyes were distinctive too, and his had held hers several times over breakfast, as they did now. It was an intimate look, meant to be reassuring, but its very intimacy was terrifying. It deepened the lie, and it was moreover so very hard not to respond to with a smile.

In the carriage, her thoughts were thus racked with guilt and fear. Beth was afraid that her sense of humour, normally her port in any storm, was deserting her.

'What was the name of that dressmaker you mentioned, my dear? The one who made your shocking dress for the masquerade?' the princess was saying.

'Madame Godot,' said Beth flatly. She realised that her listlessness was causing offence and she added, 'she is truly a marvel, I believe.' She mentally kicked herself for lack of attention. She had now confirmed the Vauxhall night to Princess Emmeline.

The princess smiled. 'Well, she sounds French at least, and all my gowns are from Paris, you know. I have wondered how I shall ever survive in London. The new English arrivals at our balls looked a trifle dowdy, my husband always thought, but I told him we were more wholesome.' She laughed.

'I secretly agreed with him. As soon as the Paris modistes had me, they made me over entirely.' Beth frowned a little at this, confused, since England had so long been at war with France. The princess laughed a little guiltily. 'Well, our tiny country was entirely neutral at the time of war, so I was free to visit Paris whenever I liked. Indeed I had to, as wife of the Crown Prince,' she added defensively.

Beth smiled. 'Of course you must have,' she attempted Miss Sophy's tone once more, 'and your pelisse is a work of art. It is so smart that every woman in London will be green with envy.'

The princess looked more comfortable. The cerulean blue pelisse with the dark green velvet epaulets and buttons was indeed sharply styled. 'I daresay they will. But in spite of everything wonderful about the continent, I shall be glad to go to Almacks again, and Vauxhall Gardens.'

'Oh,' said Beth, 'I think the ladies of the *ton* hardly dare Vauxhall at night these days, so shocking as they may be, though many enjoy the entertainments in the day time.'

The princess leaned forward, with a wicked eye, 'Well, you of all people, my dear Miss Ludgate, must know.'

Beth blushed, remembering the foul evening. 'I am not Miss Ludgate, I assure you,' she whispered near to the princess's ear.

That lady put up a pacifying hand. 'Of course you are not. You are Elizabeth, eh, Fox, is it not?'

her eyes twinkled. 'I shall call you Beth.' Beth's heart nearly stopped. How had she hit on this? Elizabeth, her given name, had so many derivatives, Eliza, Liz, Lizzie, Betty, Bess — yet she called her by her true name. She smiled, somehow her terror about being found out diminished a little at the sound of her own name. Ridiculous, but true.

'And the maid?' the princess asked.

Beth gripped her own leg in nervousness, and the royal eyes lowered.

'Oh, her leg?' Beth gazed at her interlocutor, too puzzled to follow her. 'Did she break it?' Beth blinked, which she saw the princess take as assent.

The princess chatted for some time, on different subjects, and Beth replied with smiles and the occasional phrase to keep her flow going. Part of Beth watched the princess with amusement, part with awe. She was at once sophisticated and yet revealed her youth at other times. Her life seemed to be wholly given over to pleasure, and her pleasures consisted of shopping and dancing and nothing else very sensible at all. Miss Sophy could talk of gowns of course, but she was usually too busy plotting her next clandestine excursion to give the topic more than a quarter hour, whereas the princess... Beth wondered a little at the empty-headedness, and suspected something was behind it. What, she could not imagine.

Beth sighed and tried not to think of what would become of her in London. She had only known the best addresses and the loveliest of shops whilst with Miss Sophy, and she had no notion about the other side of the city. But she feared it. Still, a job at a respectable inn. It was possible. Or perhaps she could offer her services to a dressmaker like Madame Godot. Well, perhaps not so high as that, but someone might give her a job and a cot in a backroom until she found a place. She cheered at this. She pictured herself sewing all day, and she always found pleasure with her needle. It could be a good, respectable life.

Tobias Brunswick, the Marquis of Wrexham, rode alongside the carriage often enough to hear the chatter of his sister and the occasional responses of Miss Fox, as she wished to be called. He had been clear that he had to offer his aid to the frightened young lady from the coaching inn, she seemed, for all her up-tilted chin, to be on the edge of some nervous collapse. But once in bed last night, he began to wonder, as Tennant had so phrased it, what on earth he would do with her when they arrived in London. Could he take her at her word and let her wander off to her secret rendezvous? Was London her home, or the home of friends? Had she escaped from school and was ashamed to own it? Or had she been fooled into running off with some ne'er-do-well that she was to meet in London? Or did she run away from home after a fight with her family to seek some friend in the city?

And where was her maid? He could not believe

Beth and the Mistaken Identity

the young girl had run off alone. Perhaps the tale of the maid's broken leg was true, and he could send a man back along the road to talk to her. The servant would be reluctant to break her mistress's confidence, very likely. But she must fear the girl's family more, given that they must pay her wages.

He had instructed his sister to sound out his young runaway. But Emmeline had smiled and said that she had an idea already who Miss Fox really was. That was all very well, but the miles under the horse's hooves were being eaten up and he really could not leave the girl to fend for herself in London, whatever her objections. Until he delivered her into her family's hands, he would have to keep her by him. If she would not tell them her story, it would be dashed awkward. Thank God at least that his sister would be staying with him.

And he must shut Tennant's mouth about the girl. Tennant was a casual friend from his club, who had been travelling to the same sporting event with him and had delayed his return to London in order, he thought, to spend time with his sister. The richest widow in town had been paying a brief visit to a friend in the country, and Tennant was probably glad to meet up with her, away from her admirers in London. It had done him no good, Emmi had hardly deigned to notice him over breakfast, the marquis smiled to think of it. A few hours in Mr Tennant's unrelieved company had given the marquis the resolution never to be so again. Some streams are shallow indeed.

Tennant had paid no attention at all to their mystery lady. Had not seen the kind glances she sent to those who served her, but Wrexham had, and those who served her appreciated it.

Running from school or family was not considered good behaviour amongst young ladies, whatever the cause, and he would ensure Tennant kept silent on that head. But if only his sister would talk less about herself and try to find out more about the girl, then they might jump the fence without any damage. He could deliver her to those responsible for her in London.

She was such a sweet little thing. The marquis did not see himself as having a soft heart, but something in her constant triumph over the deep fear he saw in her raised up his protective instinct. But what to do with her if she would not tell her tale was a real problem.

Though she had almost willed the horses to slow down as they approached the city, now they had entered it, Beth must leave this rather strained comfort and be on her way alone. She had made a plan, as far as she was able, to find some London inn of the respectable kind and present herself for a position. And if not, pay for a room there. But she knew that if she applied for a position and was refused, she would not afterwards be considered respectable enough to have a room at the inn. She dreaded such places as might be seen fit for a discharged maid to stay. As they passed the pillared facade of Grillon's hotel, she wondered if that orderly looking establishment might be an answer. She was sure that such a place would have an overseer quite as strict as Mr Larkins at Foster Hall, and a girl could sleep safe in her bed. But of course, the first thing that would be asked for would be her recommendation, even supposing that in this vast tumult of a city there were not another hundred young girls seeking work there. Her heart fell further into her boots. A quick prayer lifted her chin. No, an inn it would be. But first she must be untangled from the marquis's party. She was still thinking of how this might be achieved, when the carriage pulled up at a smart London square, one which she knew and had walked through as a thorough-way from General Lord Horescombe's house two miles away. They had walked through towards Bond Street, around which fashionable dressmakers and milliners plied their trade.

Miss Sophy was an energetic walker, and they had gone this way daily, her mistress haunting the shops beyond, which bored Lady Ernestine quickly and ended by Sophy being allowed to go along with only her maid. Miss Sophy chattered endlessly with Beth, but soon encountered friends of her own, and Beth had walked behind with other attendants, not permitted to converse themselves. It was always a relief. Miss Sophy was quite capable of giving a passing young gentleman such a shy, maidenly smile as to cause him to follow her, or to drop her reticule or twist her ankle, or any number of such things that might allow the gentleman to speak to her without introduction. This set Beth's teeth on edge, for her duty as attendant was to stop strange gentlemen approaching her charge, but she could do little in this case but stay close to Miss Sophy, despite hints to take herself off. Listening and watching one of Miss Sophy's London acquaintances, a Miss Oaksett, making flirtatious advances to such bucks as they encountered, Miss Sophy had once said to her, 'She is gentlemen mad!' And Beth had understood, suddenly, that Miss Sophy was not. She was mischief-mad. The gentlemen were tools to further her ends.

Now, as she stepped down from the coach, aided by the marquis's strong hand, she began her practised speech. 'Oh thank you so much your lordship, I am very near my destination now, and I will say goodbye to you and Her Royal — I mean Serene Highness.' (*The princess had corrected her on the journey, saying, 'Is it not absurd, as though I have ever been serene in my life.'*)

The marquis grasped her hand more firmly.

'Oh, I shall call a maid and we shall accompany you to your family home.'

'But I do not at all need you to!' said Beth rather desperately.

'Nevertheless, your family would never forgive a gentleman who left a young lady to walk home alone.'

'It is but a step, I assure you ...'

Beth and the Mistaken Identity

'A neighbour, then?' smiled the marquis looking down at her kindly, 'It is even more imperative.'

'Perhaps you could just summon a maid,' said Beth with an assumption of good manners. 'You need not trouble to attend me yourself.'

'Ah!' laughed the marquis, 'It would be easier to give the maid the slip, would it not?' He was teasing her and Beth trembled with weariness, and the need for freedom, but he had not yet let go of her hand. Something in his smile evoked one in hers. She had never met such a man.

'No, my lord. I just—'

'Might I suggest,' said the princess, 'that we have this discussion indoors? It is most frightfully cold.' She too smiled at Beth, 'You may as well agree, my dear Miss Fox. My brother can be kind, but desperately ruthless when he wants his way.'

So Beth was handed up the steps of the great house by the marquis himself, trembling violently. She stood stock-still in the square hall, almost reaching out to take the princess's pelisse before she could stop herself. The quick French maid stepped in before this catastrophe could occur and soon she found herself, in spite of the protests she had given, divested of her own pelisse and bonnet. She watched as the marquis made a remark of recognition to his butler whom he called Dow, but strode past a curtsying maid without really seeing her. It was another blow to her conscience. This is the true significance of a maid, not being led into an elegant sitting room and offered refreshments.

The marquis seemed to take in her appearance, without doing the ungentlemanly thing of drawing his eyes over her. She was wearing Miss Sophy's blue dress with the double frills carefully unpicked to make it plainer, and a gathered muslin insert above the neckline making it rather more decorous than when Miss Sophy wore it. The problem had once more been that the gathered bodice fell rather lower on Beth's plump bosom than on Miss Sophy's.

She found herself alone with the marquis, the princess having gone upstairs to see the safe disposal of Trixie, the snapping Pekingese, whom she declared out of sorts because she was exhausted.

'My dear girl, you must not be afraid of me,' said the marquis, coming rather closer to her and looking down with his strange sapphire eyes. She looked up and blinked, suddenly knowing how young girls could fall so far from grace. It was, at this time of high stress and near panic about her future life, like a Morpheus drug to be looked on with such care and attention by a man whose strong shoulders might bear any of her burdens. She supposed Mrs Shuttleworth would call him a worldly temptation. He smelled of horseflesh and some spicy soap. If she were a pretty piece and he showed some interest in her beyond his fatherly demeanour at the moment, she might throw herself into his arms and weep, unburdening herself of all worldly, and probably heavenly, concerns.

Beth and the Mistaken Identity

And take whatever consequences accrued.

'Please tell me how I can help you. I expect your worries might be less serious than you think. If you confided them to me, or perhaps my sister, we could aid you in sorting out whatever they may be. Your family would be glad to have you restored.'

'I have no family!' said Beth automatically. The Family — the Fosters were always referred to in this way by their household — were no longer hers. And everyone else was far away. She blinked, unable to stop two large tears escaping her eyes. She did not mean to say that, and she did not know how to respond to his kindness. Could she risk the truth and see his disgust as he cast her from the room? His eyes were still on hers, and he looked with compassion on her. His hand touched her face where the tear fell, and he said, 'Poor child!'

The princess, entering the room at this interesting moment, said, 'Miss Fox, Beth, come with me so that we may tidy ourselves a little before we have refreshments. Your hair has fared no better than mine under your bonnet, I'm afraid.'

Beth said, 'Of course!' glad to be free of the spell of the marquis's eyes and the hot sensation that remained where his finger had trailed.

As they mounted the stairs together, the Princess said, 'My brother is a hard case, and you have broken him! I am *so* impressed, Miss Ludgate!'

'I am not—' said Beth desperately. They had reached a door, and the princess swept her in, nodding to the elderly but elegant French maid to exit. 'If I had any doubts before, your capture of my careful brother would be evidence indeed. Miss Sophy Ludgate, not yet fully come-out, is already famous for entrapping the town's most eligible, but entrenched, bachelors. And now my brother, the fascinating Tobias — with his broken heart ensuring that he never gives any young lady cause to think him enamoured. And I find him, within a day of meeting you, touching your face.'

There was a great deal of misinformation to pick up in this speech, but Beth could not help herself by picking on the most intriguing. 'Broken heart?'

'Then you haven't heard of Wrexham's scandal? He was engaged six years ago to Lady Mary Ponsonby. She was pretty, vivacious and audacious, but she ran away with Bertie Lawrence —' then, as Beth looked blank, 'you know, the lecherous Earl! I suppose the scandal was rather before your time.' She shrugged. 'Anyway, since then, Toby will have none of any lady.' Suddenly she laughed. 'Oh, how delicious...' as Beth looked blank once more, 'How did I *just* describe Lady Mary?'

Beth said, distractedly, 'Pretty, vivacious and audacious.'

'You see?' said the princess, still laughing, 'Just as the famous Miss Sophy Ludgate has been described to me. As well as a naughty minx.'

Beth could think of a few more words to describe Miss Sophy. 'If I *were* she, and I am *not*, how could you wish your brother to show interest in someone liable, by your description, to cause him pain?'

'Do not be offended, my dear Sophy — may I call you so? — Toby's heart has been so long locked in his chest that it needs an airing! Perhaps meeting you is just what he requires.' As Beth looked appalled, she added, 'Not for long, of course. You must promise me not to lead him too far, but perhaps it will be an exercise to let him join the world of women once more. Look at how you affected the reclusive Mr Forster. My friend Maria Sutcliffe informed me of all the latest *on dits* by letter, so you must not think my two years a princess makes me quite out of touch. Anyway, Maria told me how Mr Forster came to a number of tedious musical evenings, only to see you. But after all he met Miss Stavely, who plays so brilliantly, and offered for her. If you had not dragged him from his seclusion, how could that have prospered?'

Shaking herself from the recollection of how this had occurred, Beth asked the princess, 'Does your brother, then, hold himself in seclusion?'

'No, no. Why, Wrexham may be found everywhere, even Almacks, escorting our cousins, at times. It is just that he does not seem to *see* the young girls around him, not as possible brides, at least. He dances with his family and with married ladies, and seems perfectly content. How he behaves with creatures of another class I could not say!' The princess laughed, but stopped when she saw something in Beth's eyes. 'I should not talk so with you. Indeed, I know nothing of Toby's amusements. Only that men have them, you know.'

Beth, who had been both furious and scared by the mention of lower class females, was now moved by something in the princess's eyes. Perhaps her prince had not been faithful, but took his pleasure elsewhere. There was hurt in the princess's eye, and Beth, whose hands were still in her grasp, squeezed slightly. Her Serene Highness blinked and smiled brightly. 'Besides, I like you already, Soph— very well, Beth! — and I do not believe you would hurt my brother. Whatever your reputation you are not considered cruel! But do tell me, how on earth did you entice Mr Forster from his home, which not the most insistent matchmaking mama could breach?'

Beth remembered precisely how Miss Sophy had managed it. As they were walking through the park, Miss Oaksett had pointed out a gentleman. She named him as the wealthy Mr Forster, who had held out against the invitations of mamas desirous of introducing their daughters. On that occasion Miss Sophy had said, 'A trifle fusty, but he shows promise!' about the tall figure of Mr Forster, handsome, Beth considered, but rather more simply dressed than the usual town beaus.

Miss Sophy then shamelessly followed him to a music emporium, Beth believing that the only thing to make this better for her mistress might be veiled bonnets or kerchief masks. Beth herself worried about being discovered in this completely improper situation, knowing that however fair Lady Ernestine and the earl could be, the maid would ultimately be held responsible. But how was Beth to stop these starts of Miss Sophy's? She concluded that Lady Ernestine had no more notion than she, so all she could do was stick close to her and hope for the best.

The gentleman evidently perused the shelves and instruments for some little time before he emerged, carrying a parcel which could be deduced as sheet music, and then he dispatched his servant, within their hearing, to buy tickets for a new concert of Mr Handel's work, which the shopkeeper had informed him of.

Later, Lady Ernestine was easily persuaded to purchase tickets, perhaps believing that Miss Sophy's thoughts were been given a more proper direction. After the concert Miss Sophy had described to Beth how she had twice passed Mr Forster's box, fortuitously on the ground floor — never once paying him attention, but hoping that he saw her in her prettiest silver dress, with silver butterflies in her hair. As Miss Oaksett, who had also accompanied them, had prattled on, Miss Sophy had interrupted her and said, 'But the music, my dear Miss Oaksett, have you not been moved by the heavenly music?' just as they had passed Mr Forster's box.

The next week, in the park once more, Miss Sophy's fall had been well timed, too. Mr Forster had no option, as Beth helped Sophy to her feet, to pick up her scattered music pages and said, as though his memory was vaguely jogged, 'Handel!' He looked at her more closely.

'Thank you sir!' fluttered Miss Sophy, with lowered eyes.

Beth brushed off leaves from Miss Sophy's pelisse, but responded to a nip on her shoulder and stood behind her a little way.

'The name is Forster, ma'am. I trust you are unhurt!'

'Oh yes, Mr Forster. It is only my fingers I care about, I'm afraid. I shall need to practise my piece. And Mr Handel is a challenge, however passionately I feel about his music.'

Beth silently agreed.

Mr Forster looked suddenly struck. 'Do you have a silver dress?'

Miss Sophy laughed. 'You do not mean you were at last week's concert?'

'I was.' There appeared on the severe face of Mr Forster what might pass for a smile. 'What did you think of Mr Latimer's performance? I thought he had rather heavy handed underscoring of the counterpoint. I found it drowned out the more flowing Italian style to the piece. In other performances, it has been, I believe, more balanced, more true to Mr Handel's intention.'

'I do not think myself qualified to discuss such subtleties with you, Mr Forster. I only play.' And

Miss Sophy accompanied this with her most shy and captivating smile. Beth stepped forward a little as Mr Forster smiled more fully.

'Miss Sophy, Lady Ernestine is expecting you at the Subscription Library.'

'Oh, yes, Beth. Quite right.' Miss Sophy cast down her eyes in a picture of shyness. 'Thank you sir. It was a pleasure to meet another music lover.' She turned away, but Mr Forster called to her.

'Where will you perform, Miss Ludgate?'

'Oh, only at Lady Carston's musical soiree, sir.'

'Ah,' he said and bowed.

Miss Sophy curtsied and Beth breathed more easily as they had walked off. She was already dreading tomorrow's walk, for whatever mischief it might bring.

What precisely Miss Sophy had wanted from Mr Forster she had never fully explained to Beth. Certainly she had enjoyed her friend Miss Oaksett's amazement at her achievement in drawing the rich bachelor into society. And she'd talked to Beth of his attention to her at the first and second musical soirees. However, Miss Sophy's mastery of the pianoforte was non-existent. Indeed, when she attempted to practise a Handel piece to make good her boast, her fingers on the keys sounded like a herd of escaped horses.

Miss Sophy had said to Beth, who was tidying nearby, 'What did you think, Beth?'

'Very nice, miss.'

'Tell me the honest truth. I order you!' said Miss

Sophy with her dancing eyes.

'Well miss, it sounded like the bag of cats Peter caught last week.'

Miss Sophy grinned, and it was only necessary for an application of a muslin bandage on her wrist, applied by Beth and tied with the prettiest of ribbons, to attest to her inability to play, due to strain. But after two soirees, Mr Forster's musical conversation had palled and Miss Sophy could no longer feign rapture at the music.

Indeed, even Mr Forster himself had been disgusted with many performances, 'If society must foist their daughters on us to display their musical talent, could not they first be assured that they have talent to display?' And then Miss Stavely had sat down (*"With her orange hair and freckles!"* said Miss Sophy) and he had been entranced. 'And instantly in love,' had said Miss Sophy to Beth, with disgust. 'Even though she had the poorest complexion of any girl I have ever seen.' Beth had removed the pins from her mistress's hair and silently cheered for Miss Stavely.

Looking now at the princess, smiling as naughtily as Miss Sophy, Beth tried not to lie. 'I am not Miss Ludgate, you really must believe me!'

Sophy Ludgate was in her room in General Lord Horescombe's house, a fine Elizabethan manor, almost unique in surviving that old fire of London, (being fortunately enclosed from its path by two streams and a priory wall) and looking at the rich but old fashioned furnishings with disdain. What was the penchant in past times for heavy tapestries and furniture it would take several strong men to move? It gave one a feeling of depression and Sophy was not prone to depression.

'You'll be glad of the heavy curtain come nighttime, these windows let in the cold,' said her prosaic cousin Ernestine, when Sophy had said as much.

Ernestine was dark and would have been pretty if she were to take more care of her appearance, thought Sophy. If there was a ball, or a formal dinner party in Horescombe House, she did indeed put on a dress (chosen for her by her lady's maid on a shopping trip) that was elegant, and had her hair styled in a more elaborate manner — and she looked very well indeed. But she abhorred furbelows and spending time on her toilette and was as often in her grandmama's cloak and sturdy boots than in the simple but elegant pelisses her lady's maid saw to it that she owned. She had many simple cambrics in brown or grey, and her maid suffered and made her hair up simply into a knot, which escaped in curls at will. But Ernestine was never ignored, however plain her clothes and eccentric her style. She did not care what others thought of her, and although never rude to those who did not cross her, she was perfectly able to give a set down at will. Sophy liked her refusal to conform, and that had made them almost friends when she had first arrived in London. Ernestine did what she wanted, but Sophy had come to realise that this was a privilege of her rank. Her grandfather was an earl, after all, and she herself was very wealthy, which had ensured her independence. Sophy too would be rich one day, if not as rich as her guardian. But until then, she was expected to tow a line not of her own choosing. Sophy did not waste time being angry about this, merely kept alert to notice how to assert her own will.

'But the earl is rich. You might have elegant furniture in the style of Mr Adam.' She brightened up. 'Oh, I know! We could redecorate the house, choose some handsome pieces together.'

Ernestine had kicked a solid chest, saying, 'What is the need of change? This was built to last.'

'Unlike the leaky windows,' said Sophy.

'Well, leaky or not, they have stood the test of time.'

'Don't you want the house to look more fashionable, when visitors come?'

Ernestine regarded her as though she were a strange animal. 'No,' she said, and left.

There was no trying to persuade Ernestine, Sophy had tried before. But the good news was that she was now in London, and that gave Sophy many things to think about. The presence of the old busybodies from Appleby village, the Misses

Fosdykes, was a hurdle. Not so much the tedious old windbag Miss Wilhelmina, but her sister Miss Florencia was a tartar of the first order, with an eye like an eagle for improper behaviour. Because of their status as distant relatives, they had been invited to keep an eye on Sophy at Foster Hall, and visited often. As one of the genteel families of the area, they had also attended the meagre entertainments, and frequently mentioned, Miss Wilhelmina delicately and Miss Florencia bluntly, some minor infractions in behaviour. *May I just give you a hint, Miss Ludgate, as I'm sure you are too kind to be otherwise aware, that I believe you wounded Miss Prendergast's feelings by talking so long to her affianced husband.* (Miss Wilhelmina), and *You talked with Mrs Brand of Mr Ward's corpulence. Do not.* (Miss Florencia).

After the dismissal of her maid Beth, Sophy had had an interview with Miss Fosdyke that she would not soon forget. Somehow it was as though something dreadful had occurred and that she, Sophy, was selfish not to think of the harm she had done. It was just that she was fusty and old, and even Lady Foster had been entertained when she had heard from Sophy the details of the reprimand. 'Well,' she had said, 'to talk so much of the maid! I thought she would ring a peal over *your* head about the risks to your person and your reputation that you take with your shocking behaviour.' Sophy had heard a great deal on this head already and yawned. 'To be sure,' said her ladyship, 'it is both an annoyance and an inconvenience to lose a maid, but after that evening she could hardly be trusted.' Yet it was Miss Florencia's words that had caused her a pause. Only for a minute, it was true, for she knew that she had been very generous to her maid in many ways and more affectionate than other, more selfish young ladies. Beth had been the nearest to her in age in the whole of Foster Hall, and she had made a friend of her. She quite missed her now. Making up plans for entertainment, and evading detection, was better done with someone who listened as well as Beth. If she was ever applied to, she would defy Lady Foster and write her a handsome character. If only the recipient did not know her ladyship's signature. One bored day, Sophy had practised it, observing to her ladyship that it would be easier for her if Sophy also *signed* the invitations she sent out (for her boring card parties or stultifying dinners) to spare Lady Foster the fatigue. Her ladyship had sent her a sharp look, but was so lazy that she agreed, even instructing Sophy on the correct flourish that she gave at the end of her name.

But after the move to London, it was unlikely that Beth would know where to apply. Oh, well.

Chapter 5

'She is *exactly* who I said she was!' said the princess to her brother.

'She has confided in you at last?' said Wrexham, looking up from his position. He was leaning forward on the tall mantelpiece with one hand and kicking at a log with a very expensive boot.

'As good as!'

Wrexham looked askance. 'She must tell us who to send her to, or she will become a very awkward permanent visitor. I may have to get a good deal harsher. I would already if she didn't seem so terrified.' He sighed, 'I don't suppose you know anything at all about it, Emmi.'

Emmeline looked at her brother's scornful face, wanting, as she once had as a child, to squash his nose with her fist. 'I tell you I do! *And* I know the reason she's run away from home.'

'From school, I thought.'

'No, I think our young Beth is rather older than she looks. Indeed, I believe she is about to be presented next season.'

'Stop taking the pig for a walk, Emmi, and tell me what you know before she comes down to dinner.'

'Oh, she won't. She is too afraid that you will ferret out her secret and be disappointed in her as her family probably is!'

'She told me she had no family.'

'Oh, that is right, I think, as far as it goes. She was orphaned at an early age and she's been looked after by the Horescombes, who are some distant kind of relatives, I believe.'

'Really? Old Horescombe and Lady Ernestine have a young girl in their care? I should not have thought them best suited for the task. The general's a recluse these days and if Ernestine Horescombe has any interest beyond books, I have yet to learn of it. And I have never seen them together.'

'Well why should you? The girl's not out yet.'

'So beyond it being a remarkably dull house for a young lady, why *has* Miss Fox run away from the Horescombes?'

'Well,' said the princess, considering, 'I *could* take a really good guess, but it would involve telling you of a childish recklessness that you might not quite approve of.'

'If I can survive your pranks, Your Serene Highness, I suppose I might be lenient to any of that sweet girl's.'

Emmeline looked at him speculatively. Would it be counterproductive to her cause of opening her brother's heart by the tool of the young girl's sweet face to tell him about her indiscretion? On balance, she thought it would show her vivacity of spirit. Like his old love, Lady Mary's.

'Well, what sin has Miss Fox committed that has led to her feeling the need to run from the Horescombes?'

'Vauxhall Gardens! That is where I knew her from. She was wearing a most daring pink dress and she and the young lady with her seemed to be enjoying themselves hugely. And I wish you would stop calling her Miss Fox. Her real name is Sophy Ludgate, and Maria has told me some tales of her daring, I assure you.

Her brother looked more shocked than she had judged likely. 'Vauxhall Gardens — at a ball there? I would not have believed it of her.'

Emmeline made haste to explain. 'Well, but it is not so *very* bad. Just a simple childish prank. She must have been made to suffer afterwards, by the state of play now.'

'We must send to the general now. The Horescombes must be frantic with worry.'

'Yes, but I think she might be better to stay here tonight, do you not? I had a tray sent to her room and her bed made ready and told her she must rest and we will deal with everything in the morning. We can let the Horescombes know she is safe for tonight.'

'But what if she runs away? How could we make *that* up to the general?' The marquis pretended a shudder, 'He's a tartar when crossed.'

'We'll put a footman outside her room or some such thing.'

The thought of Miss Fox, or Miss Ludgate, being above stairs gave Wrexham a different kind of shiver, but still he agreed. He wrote a letter to the Earl of Horescombe and gave it to Dow, 'To be sent on the moment, Dow.'

Sitting in her chamber, where a friendly fire had been made up and a hot brick had been placed between the sheets, she had no idea what to do next. She was warm and safe tonight, at least, if not at ease. If she dropped her guard, she would find herself in Newgate Prison, and this was probably where she belonged. Lying was becoming a way of life to a girl so strictly brought up. The maid who had brought her supper tray and had turned down the bed had been nervous in her presence. Fear of complaint perhaps. She wondered if Mr Dow the butler, or Dow as she should call him now she was in the role of lady, was as fair to the household as Mr Larkins had been to her. Of course, it had been Mrs Badger, the housekeeper at Foster Hall who had been her superior, but Beth knew that it was a butler who gave a house its tone. The girl's fear, in the presence of so lowly a guest as she, said that something was not quite right, unless of course she was *very* new.

Beth and the Mistaken Identity

Almost subliminally, Beth had noticed some things out of alignment with a well-run home. On the upper floor, this marquis's magnificent home had some dust in places Mrs Badger, the housekeeper at Foster Hall, would not have tolerated. But it was more than that. She might give herself time to think about it, if it was any of her business.

The young maid, perhaps sixteen, had asked if she wished to be undressed and Beth had almost laughed. She had never been helped to dress in her life, beyond the age of about four. Her mama had no time to dress children. She turned away, though, and said merely, 'That will not be necessary, Aggie, thank you.'

She had been just such a servant in a fine country house. Had, unlike many others, stayed faithfully in her place and had worked her way up to being a lady's maid, by great diligence and skill, to the young lady of that family. Miss Sophy was not at all a strict mistress. On the contrary, she was affectionate and kind, and as a young lady of fashion, a credit to the attentions of her maid. If sometimes she did not understand that a velvet cape whose lining had been torn and stained could not be mended (for it required to be completely relined) for a ball the next evening — well, that was perfectly natural. It was essential for the smooth running of a house, had said Mr Larkins the butler, to have their labours be invisible to the Quality at all times. So Beth had sat up all night and sacrificed her only half-day that month to be certain it was done as her mistress required.

Mr Larkins had noticed, as he noted everything that happened in the house, and had nodded to her in a way that made her heart swell with pride. Mr Larkins was a deity to Beth. Her mother had been in service with him twenty years ago, and had written to him (for she too had risen to the heady heights of lady's maid, and knew her letters) and had known that he kept an orderly house above and below stairs. The hierarchy was more strictly observed below than above stairs. No young pot boy or footman would offer her an insult of any kind, and relations between the servants was strictly forbidden. The position was everything her mother could wish for her. She sent home money every quarter day, and it added to her mother's meagre income from the farm.

Now, with another five children to care for, the Widow Culpepper would miss that money grievously.

She could go home, of course, but she had visited once since she'd had her position and she was not quite fitted to the life anymore. She could still milk a cow and harness the plough horses, but she had annoyed her mother with her new found 'finicky ways'. She washed all the children's clothes and held each of her brothers and sisters under the pump, and her mother had told her off for wasting time. 'And don't look at me as though you wish to wash me too, Elizabeth Culpepper, or I'll slap your face for you.' Her mother was her

Beth and the Mistaken Identity

heroine, and Beth had been very sad to make her feel belittled, but when one's job for seven years had been in the service of cleanliness and order, it was difficult not to bring this home to the farm. Her mother had forgiven her, having once suffered from the same time-wasting obsessions, before life on a farm with Ned Culpepper and their children had changed her priorities.

Her sister Nessie had promised Beth (secretly) to wash the little ones every Friday night and to keep herself as neat as she could. But after that visit, Beth knew that quite apart from being another mouth to feed, she could never return to that home to live. Jem, her brother, was more diligent than her Pa, but at sixteen he still only earned a few shillings from other farmers, as well as growing and tending what fed them on their own tenancy, which he had taken over from his dead pa. Between Jem and Nessie, Mother had borne only dead babes, for Ness was but eleven, with Maisie at eight, John at six and little Theodore at four, by which time Pa had (fortunately) died. It may be a sin to think so, but there could be no doubting that Mother and Jem had done better without him, his drinking, and his inconsistent working of the farm. The farm profits were eaten up by the rent. Nessie would be off to service in a year or so, but until then, any actual money, beyond some pennies for eggs or milk sold, came from the wages of Beth. She needed to make sure she could replace them soon.

She must get away from these solicitous captors and begin to make a new path for herself. As Beth snuggled beneath the warm sheets she sat up and sipped the hot milk that had been left for her, suddenly finding it all so funny. The luxury of this room, with the silken coverlet, the fine linen, the pretty paper on the walls, the gilded furniture and ceiling. A marquis and a princess calling themselves her friend. She laughed. Yesterday morning Lady Foster had cast her out. If she thought of her fate at all, she might suppose her sleeping in some flea-ridden lodgings. Certainly not a friend of royalty, sleeping in a canopied bed. It was sinful not to give thanks for God's mercies, after all. She leaned back on the goose down pillows, determined to enjoy this one night when she might be as surrounded in luxury as Marie Antoinette.

But everyone knew what had happened to her...

Chapter 6

Beth awoke in the night. She was restless, having just had her head lopped off as she slept, and decided to go in search of a book, having seen a library off the tall, square entry hall. Perhaps, if she read and did not go back to sleep, a little later she might leave before the house arose: she was too afraid of walking the streets of London in the pitch dark. This last resolve seemed doomed, for there was a liveried footman in the hall, sprawled in a chair sleeping. She could get past him in bare feet, but was quite sure he had been set to make sure she did not leave the house. A prison indeed.

She slid into the library and longingly looked around the shelves, trailing her fingers across the book spines, as she had done frequently in Foster Hall. She had read there too, taking books and hiding behind a large chair, curled up to read without being seen. To borrow them and take them to her room was to court disaster. Books were expensive, after all, and to be found with one would be theft. In the servants' attics, there were too many people who could find out about her occupation. She had been taught her letters by her mama at an early age, as had all the children. Strangely, her father had not objected to this, since he had some pride in his heritage (that might be descried in the pages of an old family Bible) some ancient relatives of his being landed gentry. Her mother had held, in this one instance, that reading was necessary to know one's scripture. But she had still let Beth read other tales, some that her mother possessed and hid against being sold by her father. There were others that the vicar lent her, and so she had grown in her love of books.

She was especially adjured to keep silent about this, for to be educated above one's station was still prohibited with some masters. It made servants rebellious and unfitted for their station, it was held, and they should know as little of one's business as possible. Of course, in reality, servants knew everything between them, and that was irrespective of their ability to read, Beth had discovered. But upper servants were sometimes taught, for the convenience of their betters, and Beth had contrived to make Miss Sophy think, without lying precisely, that she had been an excellent teacher, and that Beth had learnt only from her young mistress, in case she be thought presumptuous in her learning. Even when Beth had read for two hours in the short night-time permitted a servant, she'd thought herself almost more refreshed than when she only slept.

Now, among the handsome leather Latin volumes (Beth had not mastered Latin, unfortunately) she found a copy of *Robinson Crusoe*, which her mother also possessed. She greeted it as a friend, and took it down avidly, almost heading for a place behind a chair. But then she realised that her position as guest gave her some privileges, so she sat *on* the chair instead. She was able to extinguish her candle and read by the dying embers in the fire, which warmed her.

In ten minutes or so, she was quite engrossed, when a candle spilt some light on the carpet, as a man entered. She saw by the glittering braid on his uniform that it was the footman from the hall. He did not perceive her, and moved towards a tray on a side table, and poured himself a glass of amber liquid. At first frozen, Beth stood up, letting the book fall to the floor.

The candlelight covered her and a voice behind it said 'Miss!' There was fear in that voice, and it showed Beth her power. Mr Larkins had very strong views on servants drinking and she was outraged, so that even when his voice became more insolent, Beth remained so. 'Miss, I was bringing his lordship a nightcap—'

'And tasting it to boot, I see. What is your name?'

'George, Miss.'

'Well, George. I think Mr ... I think Dow would be very disappointed in what I have just witnessed.'

George let a short laugh escape him. 'Yes, Miss.'

But he sounded unconcerned, insolent still. Feigning servility.

'I know the *marquis* would be.'

His tone changed. 'If you could avoid disturbing the marquis with this, Miss ... I was just a bit cold in the hall, and wanted to warm myself, miss.'

'With the master's French Brandy. It is not right, George.'

'No, Miss'

'Why did you laugh when I said I would tell Dow?'

'I didn't laugh, Miss.'

'Oh, so I may wake up the marquis ...'

'Please Miss ...! Mr Dow's partial to the brandy himself miss. Upon occasion.'

The things she'd noticed in her short visit made her enquire, 'Is Mr — is Dow a good butler?'

George looked shifty, 'He's a very accomplished —'

'Yes, yes,' said Beth dismissively, cutting short his speech. 'But what is his temper with the other servants?'

George, his handsome face gazing down at this little lady's with something approaching trust, decided on a sliver of openness. 'Variable, Miss. Very variable.'

'Is he lax?'

'Lax and a tyrant at once, I'd say.' He regarded her closely, but did not discern any threat to him in her manner. Indeed, she seemed to have suspected something of the truth, though how, he could not guess. He added a little. 'If this house were a ship, mutiny would be brewing.'

Beth put her head to one side. 'Has he been here long?' Something told Beth this could not be possible. George shook his head. 'And before Dow? Who was the butler then?'

'That was Wright, Miss. And he was a right 'un. Begging your pardon, Miss. Worked for the Family for years and ran a superior household, if you know what I mean. Now the housekeeper and Cook are at each other's throats, the maids are terrified, and Dow has dismissed three footmen in the last month.'

Beth looked at him aghast. 'Then why do you take such a risk as to—?'

He shrugged. 'It doesn't matter, much, Miss. The footmen aren't dismissed for any *particular* purpose. Just according to Mr Dow's constitution that day.' Beth shook her head in wonder. George grew serious. 'If Mr Wright were still here, Miss, I'd never—'

'Yes, I see,' said Beth, and she thought she did.

A noise disturbed them, and another candlelight entered before the marquis, dressed in only a shirt, breeches and boots. He looked from Beth to the footman and she felt compelled to say, 'Thank you George, you may give that to me and leave.'

The footman froze for a fraction of a second before saying, 'Yes miss,' and handing her the generous glass of brandy, departed soundlessly.

'Miss Fox! I beg your pardon.'

Beth noticed the strong column of his throat, rising from his open necked shirt, and strove to be calm. 'I must beg yours, sir. I came down merely to find a book. I found myself unable to sleep.'

'I am on the same errand.'

She held the glass uncomfortably. 'George asked if he could get me something and seeing the brandy there, I presumed to ask for a glass.' The marquis's eyebrows rose. 'It was a - a - habit of mine to have a glass with my father in the evening.'

'Was it?' his eyebrows rose, and he grinned. 'How unusual!' he gestured gallantly at the glass, 'Do carry on.'

Beth lifted the strong spirits to her lips and took a sip. Her eyes watered and her throat burned, but beyond a slight croak, she made no fuss.

The marquis came forward and took it from her. 'I'm sorry, I'm afraid I was teasing you. Did you find the footman dipping into my brandy?' he smiled at her, amused. 'I will have to see about that...'

'Oh, do not, I beg,' she said, her face flushed. 'I would not want to be the means to have a man dismissed.'

'You will not be. A warning only will suffice.'

He stepped aside after she smiled at him and opened the door, which he had made sure remained ajar in the name of propriety, even wider to let her pass. She stopped opposite him and looked up at his cleft chin. 'Do you know how long

Beth and the Mistaken Identity

George has been with you?'

'Well, no. Should I?' He was surprised to see what passed for anger in her eyes and gave himself to think. 'I believe he may have been quite young when he joined us, perhaps fourteen.'

Her face lost the angry look. She looked at him frankly, and pushed herself on to speak. 'Many years, then. When servants behave loosely, it is as well to look at the head of the house.'

'Myself?' he replied, still amused.

From the perspective of a servant, there was only one head of a house, the steward (but many houses no longer possessed such) or the butler. It took her a moment to say, 'The head of household, I should say.'

'Dow?'

She cast down her eyes. 'I should say no more, my lord, it is not my business. I apologise for mentioning it.'

She slid past him then, and he noticed that her night rail had been mended more than once. Miss Sophy's disguise complete, if his sister was correct. But she did not appear to him to be the hoydenish, forward young lady his sister described. She seemed quiet. Yet it *had* been forward to mention the running of the house when you were but one night a guest. He rather approved of her kindness to the footman, though he had no idea why she would put herself to the trouble. It was not as though he were her old retainer, like his servants in the country were to him, many of them were his childhood friends.

He'd liked her from the first: she was quietly pretty — not a showy filly, but there was both bravery and fear in those melting brown eyes. At first, he'd thought her a mere child, despite the plump bosom, but now he thought she had rather more years behind her than the fifteen or so he'd judged. Why that disturbed him, he did not know.

It was some time before he bethought himself of Dow. True, things did not run as smoothly as in Wright's day, and the household bills recently had risen, so his man of business had mentioned. But it was nothing he chose to worry about. However, dipping the brandy might be the thin edge of an unknown wedge. He supposed, he thought drearily, he must look into it.

Chapter 7

Beth's nervous exhaustion after encountering the marquis with the dark blue eyes and that strong cleft chin had betrayed her. She had fallen asleep in the down bed, and slept until the scared young maid opened the curtains.

Beth sat up, cursing that she had to choose this night, of all in her life, to sleep past dawn. She had lost her opportunity to make an early escape. As the maid placed a pillow behind her and handed her a tiny cup of chocolate to waken her, she wondered if something in her did not really *wish* to escape this gilded cage. She sat back and watched as the maid laid out her second gown, already having tended to her travel-stained dress and pelisse of yesterday.

'Thank you,' said Beth, wishing to give the girl some guidance on the correct placement of the gown on the chair, and thinking of some way to dismiss her without being dressed. She could think of none however, so when she finished the chocolate (whose dregs she had sipped before, only when Miss Sophy or Lady Foster had not quite finished their own) she got up and washed at the jug and ewer of hot water, using the rose scented soap provided, and submitted to being undressed and redressed in a fine shift (also Miss Sophy's reject) short stays (which the maid regarded strangely, as they were made of rough linen) and a rose-sprigged muslin that Beth would have kept for best, had not it been churlish to argue with the maid. It was a deal easier to have another person button the small buttons at the back. When Beth had the leisure, she would change these pretty trinkets with a more simple to manage, laced fastening. The maid meant to dress her hair, too, and Beth submitted. She was a trifle rough, and Beth squeaked a little, sparking the frightened look once more.

'My curls will have knotted themselves, Aggie, so it is best to go slowly,' offered Beth gently.

She was rewarded by seeing the young girl's flush abate. 'Yes, miss. Sorry miss.'

As the maid worked on her hair, Beth's brain was back to churning. It would make her soft to stay even one more night in a place where she went to sleep and awoke in a fire-warmed room, a feather bed and every luxurious thing to see. The marquis had handed her Robinson Crusoe as she left, so kind was he in his attentions. *Was* he simply kind, or was there something else in his manner? She hardly knew. Beth had met gentlemen of the aristocracy before, but had studiously avoided eye contact, as her position demanded. Young Maria Brass (and she had some, said Mrs Badger) a maid at neighbouring Hedgewick Manor, had been led to a life of sin (which sounded quite dreadful) by Lord Stanford, a rake, then cruelly abandoned. Which would probably happen to Beth now, had said the pious cook, Mrs Shuttleworth, after the dreadful Vauxhall adventure. Indeed, seeing the behaviour of some painted ladies, and some liberties that gentlemen took with them at Vauxhall, Beth was coming to an understanding of all the pitfalls. What, had said Mrs Shuttleworth, would become of such as Maria Brass once her youth and beauty had faded? Beth, a pious girl, was even more worried about her immortal soul. At least here she was free of being accosted. But it could not go on. At any moment she could be found out. And surely the kindness of the princess and her brother did not serve her continued lies.

At what point might she escape today? Beth's head hurt.

She looked up to her reflection in the mirror, and found that Aggie, the maid, had a genius. Her hair had been raised rather high and her natural ringlets escaped the high knot, and some had been encouraged around her face. They had been smoothed a little too, by the slightest touch of pomade, and the autumnal hair shone. It became her even better that those styles that she had contrived for Miss Sophy, and Beth was a trifle jealous at Aggie's skill.

'Can I put a ribbon in it Miss?'

'I fear all such decorations were in my trunk, which is with my maid, you know.'

'Yes miss.'

'You are truly gifted, Aggie. I don't suppose my hair has ever looked so fine.'

Aggie flushed and looked happy, and told her that the family would be at breakfast very soon.

Beth met the princess on the stairs who remarked, 'Why, you look very fresh today, my dear Miss, eh, Fox. Your hair is cunningly achieved.'

Since the princess's own hair was pleated, curled and piled in luscious coils upon her head, Beth was very pleased at this. 'It is the work of a rather gifted maid, Aggie, not me.'

'Really, I must remember her name in case my Cécile should be taken ill.'

Beth felt a hot rush of anger at this — the princess did not even know the names of those who served her! It was unjust, of course, the princess had not always lived here. Beth had never felt this way in her old position. It was somehow as if being treated so kindly by the princess and the marquis in her disguise as lady underlined how differently she would have been treated if she were known as a maid. The vast gulf between who she was thought to be and who she was, did not always make her grateful for their kindness. Or not so much as she should be: only resentful at the emptiness of it all. If she were Aggie, the princess would forget her name in a second. She had always known it to be so, so why did it raise her wrath now? She supposed her wrung-out nerves from the dismissal, deception and fear of the future was making her less charitable. Then too, it was difficult to know her place and respect it when she had been catapulted to the exalted position of guest of a marquis.

She feared, also, that her father's talk of primyjenchoor, the curse of inheritance unjustly given to but one child, and how otherwise his family should all now be living in a castle (drunken ravings) had somehow reared its ugly head within her. There must be many decedents of younger sons living in poverty like her family. Beth blamed it on no one. It was the way of the world, and even if your grandpapa had lived in a castle, it did not do to rail at the moon and fail to plant your own crops. Perhaps her father would have been better served never to know of his uninterested high-born relatives. Beth would give it no more thought now. That way led to her father's madness.

George held the door open to the breakfast room, and Beth smiled at him. In the briefest of looks, he showed his gratitude for her silence last night.

She joined the others at the table, making her face as composed as she could. Morning salutations were expressed, and the princess remarked on 'how fresh and youthful' Beth looked today. The marquis smiled and said, 'Charming', and Beth found herself smiling. Dow was serving his master, and he glanced her way. His face was impassive, but Beth wondered if the marquis had spoken to him yet. She nibbled on a roll, watched as Dow shot a glance that made a maid quake. She turned and saw that the marquis's eyes had followed hers, drawn by her attention. The maid looked nervous and flushed, and cast her eyes down. A hint of a frown crossed Wrexham's face. He met Beth's eye once more and she guided his eye to George, standing behind the princess's chair, ready to attend her. George's jaw was clenched, and a muscle worked in his face, contrary to all his training. The little blond maid was now shaking, after Dow had dropped word in her ear.

Beth exchanged a glance with the marquis. He said to Beth, 'Might I have a word with you after breakfast, Miss Fox?'

'I must go and seek my family I think, my lord,' she said apologetically.

The princess started to interrupt with, 'Oh my dear, we know—'

The marquis raised his hand. 'After breakfast!'

They retired after a strange meal, where the princess bore all the conversational burden, Beth hardly hearing her as her brain ran forward.

When all three had eaten and retired to the Chinese room, the marquis nodded his servants away and the princess led Beth to a sofa, drawing her down to sit. Beth twisted a handkerchief and the marquis took his place by the fire, his hands behind his back.

'Miss Fox. I have known from the first that you wanted to conceal your identity that you found yourself in some trouble, and now my sister has discovered your secret.' Beth's heart stopped. 'She had informed me that you are Miss Sophy Ludgate, ward of General Lord Horescombe, whom I know well.'

Beth squeaked, and the princess took her hand. 'You have nothing to fear, my dear, I assure you!'

'I should tell you, my lord, indeed I have wished to tell you from the first that —'

The marquis strode forward. 'You need not, my dear,' he said kindly. 'I sent last night to the general, hoping to restore you to your family today.' Beth jumped. 'You are frightened, but you need not be. No doubt Lord Horescombe will be cross with you, and read you a fine lecture, but he is not an unkind man, and it will soon pass.'

'It isn't that. Indeed,' said Beth, remembering the general's many kindnesses to her mistress, and to the servants, 'I know he is, but—'

'The letter was returned, however. I'm sorry to inform you that your family have left town for some days.'

Beth breathed again. Not to be sent to Newgate today, then. But her conscience was not to be borne longer. 'I am not Sophy Ludgate. You must believe me.'

'Then how,' said the princess brilliantly, 'do you know that the general is kind?'

This was her chance. She opened her mouth to try, but the full truth choked Beth. The princess was looking at her laughingly, and the marquis quite kindly. If she could just leave, she could escape seeing their disappointment. Indeed, perhaps they might not know the truth for some time.

'I am — a-acquainted with the general, but I am not Miss Ludgate, you must believe me.' She stood up with sudden decision. 'I must leave now, and return home to my real family. I - I cannot tell you who they are. I thank you for your hospitality and kindness, but please call for my bonnet and pelisse! I must go—' she tried very hard to keep the desperation from her voice, but the marquis was not deceived.

'Have the Horescombes gone in search of you? Do you know where they may be? They left only the vaguest information about their return, but the butler believes there is a regimental engagement next week which his master attends each year, and will surely return for.'

'*Please* sir, I must leave now,' said Beth. Her lie was becoming more plausible than the truth.

'My dear, I do not think it wise to try to return to Horescombe House, for there is no family member to bear you company.'

'I am not so fragile as you would believe ... Do you mean to keep me prisoner here?'

The princess laughed, 'I told you she had spirit, Toby! She has at you —'

Beth and the Mistaken Identity

The marquis took her hand in one of his and began to pat it gently. 'Miss — eh — Fox. You must see that we cannot send you out into the street while your family is from town. What would the general say to me then?'

'I am *not* Miss Ludgate. The general has no connection to me —'

But nothing would make them believe it, save the truth. And Beth wanted to disappear before they had to know this. She wondered if she could indeed go to Horescombe House, to Lady Ernestine? Her Ladyship had been casually kind — might she give Beth a character? But she knew that the Vauxhall disaster would have made even the mild Lady Ernestine angry, and the general tried to be as far from Miss Sophy's starts as was well possible, and probably had no notion who Beth was.

In the end, she agreed to take the air in the park with the princess this afternoon, after outright refusing to go shopping for an evening gown. She could *not* be more in debt to them than she was already.

Chapter 8

Whatever the Horescombes had planned for her, Sophy made no demur. She walked in the nearest square with the Misses Fosdyke rather than the park, where she might meet her friends, and listened to Miss Wilhelmina's good-natured witterings with glazed eyes but no complaint. She affected to read in the afternoon with Lady Ernestine, who finally gave in and took her shopping, but only for the accoutrements that might finish a toilette, not into the more frequented establishments where it was more likely she would meet friends. She sat quietly when visitors called on the earl or her ladyship, serving tea and behaving decorously. The first day, some of Lady Ernestine's friends were less than decorous themselves, for they included artists and writers, and seemed to have little truck with propriety. Sophy was not led astray in their presence, she behaved herself.

She entered the breakfast room to hear Miss Wilhelmina say, 'Sophy is really appreciative of the move to London, Lady Ernestine. Under the tender eye of her guardians she really has improved her behaviour. Why, I believe it could not be faulted.'

'When Sophy is being good, we must pay particular attention,' said Lady Ernestine, not looking up from reading a journal while a maid served her eggs.

'Fear not, Lady Ernestine, I am not so trusting as my sister.'

Sophy, who had stopped just outside the door frowned a little. What had the world come to when people were so mistrusting? But she put a smile on her face and entered the breakfast room.

The next day, Sophy made her plans. She realised that the maid that had been allocated to dress her was part of a supervision team. She was eagle-eyed and responded to Sophy's friendly overtures with a thin smile or a sniff. But the maid who brought her chocolate and laid the coals before the lady's maid arrived was another thing. After a conversation with the girl, Sophy persuaded her to send a letter to Jane Oakshott, arranging a meeting. At first the little maid had not wanted to accompany her on the walk which Sophy had suggested. Sophy confidingly admitted she did not much like her maid, Annie, and would much prefer to walk with her, Mary.

'Me neither miss,' agreed the maid, referring to Annie, 'but I cannot go with you, I have me duties and Mrs Higgins would have my guts for garters.

It's Annie's position to walk wif you, miss.'

Obviously the maid had no idea of the conspiracy against her, and that was in Sophy's favour.

'When is your afternoon off?' asked Sophy.

'Oh miss, it's today, but I would be right sorry to miss seeing my ma, miss.'

'What if you took just two hours of the time for a walk, and you could give your mama a sovereign afterwards?'

'Oh miss, you are right kind.'

'But best not tell the other servants, there might be a little jealousy.'

'Oh no, miss. I won't.'

'Meet me after one at the servants' entrance.'

'The servants' entrance, miss?'

'Yes, I shall go through the stillroom so as not to be seen.'

'Not seen miss?'

'By Annie. I do not want you to be blamed for accompanying me.'

Thankfully the girl was a little slow, as this was a very thin excuse. But the next day, Sophy left the Misses Fosdyke with an excuse to go to her room to freshen up before the afternoon visitors arrived. Today she would avoid them. She would plead to the household afterwards that she had really needed this outing, and that she had gone chaperoned, so no harm had come of it. They would be angry, of course, but Sophy didn't really pay attention much to other people's anger. The maid was waiting outside the staff entrance with her pelisse and bonnet and they began the walk to the park, where she had agreed to meet her friends. She felt free, and joyous for the first time since she had been back in town, almost swinging her reticule as she moved.

But then everything changed...

The afternoon of the second day, when the princess had taken Beth for an airing in the carriage, she had her first test. As the carriage had paused for the princess to talk to an old friend, Beth withdrew a little into the background, gazing idly around at the swells in their shining tall hats and well cut coats, the ladies with their parasols making colourful dots in the distance, moving in a measured way, taking their afternoon stroll. She saw, too, the duller figures of maids walk behind, and almost wished she were one of them, rather than looking down at them from the barouche. She'd known her place then.

'Darling,' she heard a drawling voice, of some friend of the princess, who had caused her carriage to be pulled up beside the barouche, and who had been chatting for some time. 'You have not introduced me to your friend.'

'Oh,' said the princess with an offhand manner, 'This is my friend Miss Fox, just arrived from her country home.'

It seemed to work, the lady paid no further attention to Beth and the talk of fashions continued. But when she left, the princess, in her impulsive way, turned to her. 'I quite see why you did not want to come out with me today. It would be very odd to be one day introduced as Miss Fox, and then when you come out, suddenly become Miss Ludgate.' The princess held up a hand at Beth's protest, '… or whatever your true name is. But you can certainly bear me company at Madame Godot's.'

'Please, *please*, Your Highness, I cannot.' Beth was shaking, for her frequent visits to that establishment with Miss Sophy meant it was hard to see how she would not be recognised. Madame was a tiny personage with piercing eyes which were sometimes humorous. She exchanged some hidden glances with the maid at some of Miss Sophy's starts, and had noticed Beth's appreciation of the construction of each gown. Some petal sleeves had caught her eye once, and she had marvelled at each overlapping petal of silk mousseline, made of two pieces sewn together with tiny stitches, turned and tucked, and sewn together to make a sleeve for an angel. Madame had smiled at her then, seeing Beth's gaping appreciation of the work involved. Madame would certainly know her.

The princess looked down at her and patted her hand. 'No, no my dear, we will not if you prefer.' She smiled her lovely smile. 'But Beth, please let me have some gowns sent over, you really cannot live in the two you have until next week, when the Horescombes return.'

But Beth shook her head, determined. If she

were not to hurt this kind princess, who was beginning, absurdly, to feel like her friend, she must be gone before she found out the truth.

The marquis was standing in the hall as they returned, taking off his coat. 'Would you join me in the library, Miss Fox? I have the need to speak to you.'

"What now?" thought Beth, but she passed him and moved into the library, removing her bonnet as she went.

The princess followed her, saying 'Can you not let us take some tea and remove our pelisses first?'

Her brother stepped in front of her. 'You may do so with my blessing, Emmi. I wish to speak to Miss Fox alone.'

'*Les convenances*?' his sister moued.

'I shall leave the door ajar, never fear.' He looked down at his sister's disapproving face. 'I have not suddenly become a rake while you were on the continent, Emmi.'

'I know,' said his sister, pertly. 'I only wish you had. I must away to the dressmakers once I have tea, so be quick.'

Beth stood trembling in the middle of the room, clasping her hands in front her, looking so much like a frightened schoolgirl that the marquis was moved to pity.

'Take a seat, my dear Miss Fox. I am not here to scold you.'

Her eyes flew to his, but she obediently sat, and he joined her on the same sofa, at a *convenable* distance. 'Miss Fox. I have just visited Lord Summerton, whom Dow provided as his character. He has lately returned from India, and his account of Dow's service differs very much from the character I had, as does his signature from that which adorned it. It is my intention to send Dow off this day, and leave him to forge another character if he can. It shall be for no house in London, I assure you.' He smiled at her as though she should be pleased.

'Sir! Please do not! It will be my fault that a man should be turned onto the street with so little thought. I could not bear it.'

'Fault? You cannot believe that I can have such a man in my house?'

'Oh, no, no! He cannot continue to run the place in the way he has. Eventually the Family — your family, I mean — would be made very uncomfortable. And the servants are all at sea. No, I can see that he should leave.' She looked at him pleadingly, 'But can you not write him a character? Can you not at least leave him the means to get another position?'

'And sign my name to a falsehood, making another house the recipient of his dubious services? You must know that I have interviewed the entire staff, and know of all his proclivities. His temper, his theft of spirits and of other things, the fear he strikes into his whole household, such that three maids burst into tears at his very name.'

'Oh, he must *know* then? If you interviewed the

staff?'

'I sent him on an unusual errand: he will return before dinner.' He looked at her. 'What I wish to know is, how did *you* see what I could not?'

Beth coloured. 'I do not know. I think that quiet people often notice what others do not.'

'Yet you have not the reputation of being quiet.'

She looked pleadingly into his sapphire eyes. Why would no one listen? In another situation, Beth's ready humour would have taken over, but not now. 'Please sir, I am not who you think me—' He reached over and patted her hand and in this proximity, Beth knew the impulse once more to throw herself into those arms and unburden herself. Fatal.

'I know. You are not Miss Ludgate and will not tell me who you are. But since the only person you *do* admit to knowing is General Lord Horescombe, and he returns at the end of the week, then he is the person with whom I feel safe to deposit you. He will know how to return you home.'

Beth's heart was racing. Perhaps, if she could manage to meet with Lady Ernestine when the family came back to town and have words with her, her ladyship might help. Miss Sophy was safe at Foster Hall, and perhaps Beth might be able to explain this ruse ... she had some days respite, at least. They would worry for her if she ran away now, this goodhearted, aristocratic brother and sister. No, she would wait until she could see Lady Ernestine, and maybe *she* could explain what a tangle Miss Sophy could make of lives, and they would not feel so betrayed at her deception. She could not hope Lady Ernestine could help her find a situation, but explaining her behaviour would salve her guilt. But something still bothered her.

'And Dow?'

'You have such a soft heart, little wren,' the marquis said and pinched her chin. She blushed, and she felt him breathe a little deeper, seeing him sit back with a surprised look on his face. He recovered however and said neutrally. 'I cannot give Dow a character. But I shall give him enough in coin to keep him for some months.'

'Perhaps enough for passage to the Americas or to India? I hear it is better there.'

The marquis looked at her strangely. 'Better?'

'More opportunity for people of — of Dow's class.'

'And now, I suppose, I must find myself a new butler. It is a trial.'

Despite herself, Beth laughed shortly. He had no idea what a real trial was. But she gave her thought to the problem. 'Frost is the under-butler, of course,' said Beth with a slight frown, having regarded this individual with narrowed eyes at the two mealtimes, 'but I feel he may be tainted with Dow's method.'

'Oh yes?' the marquis enquired, smiling.

'I fear so. He seemed to make Aggie as afraid as Dow.'

'And who is Aggie?'

Beth and the Mistaken Identity

'Why one of your chambermaids, your lordship,' said Beth, annoyed once more.

'Please call me Wrexham. And I beg your pardon, my dear,' he was mocking her a little, but she didn't quite perceive it.

'Well, Wrexham, I think that George might be a better fit.'

'The footman who stole my brandy?'

'Yes.' Beth said it seriously. 'He was trained under your former excellent butler. And he was sorry to see the household so upset. I believe he wishes to establish the order that once existed, the harmony among the staff.'

'I cannot for the life of me understand why, if things were so bad, that my valet or housekeeper (who have served my family for ever) could not have mentioned it.'

'Well, of course, the running of the house is beneath your valet's notice.' Beth informed him.

'It is?'

'Oh yes! That is how he keeps his superiority below stairs. He may not run the house, but he *is* your right hand man, and as such is above the regulation of any other servant. Therefore he refuses to acknowledge the running of the house, except in regard to carrying out his own duties. I am sure he would see that nothing impeded that, and Dow would understand this, of course.'

'I had not quite thought of that,' said the marquis, now thoroughly amused. 'And my housekeeper, Mrs Fitch, why has she not brought it up to me?'

'Well,' considered Beth, tilting her head to one side in thought, 'I have not spoken to her, but I expect that is because Dow set her against Cook, and she feared that to open the door to complaints to you was to risk a lot of dirty linen being washed in front of you.'

'I believe it is so. My interviews today were not happy ones. Indeed,' he remembered with distaste, 'Mrs Bates, the cook, burst into tears.'

'I expect she's at fault then. It is my experience that the guilty party always takes recourse in tears.'

He raised his brows, still smiling. 'You are very young to have made a study of it.'

'I am nineteen years.'

At this, some frisson seemed to overtake the marquis, some small, formally banked down fire seemed to leap to his eyes. Beth felt scalded. 'I thought you younger.'

His voice was intimate and low, and Beth, affected in some way she did not understand, returned, 'No, nineteen, past.' It was not an elegant way to phrase it, and Beth wondered if she had given herself away at last, but he did not notice.

Something hung between them, her eyes searched his for an answer, and then he pulled away, standing up as though needing the distance. 'I am so happy to have you remain with us some days, Miss Fox. Please promise me that you will not seek to leave us until the Horescombes return to town.'

Beth, unable to take her eyes from his, breathed back, 'I promise.'

He took her hand then and bowed over it formally, she stood, curtsied, and ran upstairs.

She was shaken, the touch of his hand left her shaken, as had that unexplainable look in his eye. It did not seem, in Beth's experience watching Miss Sophy and her attendant gentlemen, that he had been flirting. It was rather that she had some power over him that he did not wish. His pulling away showed this. That seemed unlikely, and maybe she was merely endowing him with her own feelings. But he had laughed at her, been thoroughly relaxed, and then the change. Fire in those eyes, and almost the same wonder that she herself felt. He was a gentleman, pulling away from a lady, and she blushed to wonder what he might have done if she had been merely a maid. That was a treacherous thought, and she must not indulge it. She could not help being glad that she moved him, and afraid, too. But men were like this, said Mrs Badger, and it was nothing to them, but much to the girls they played with. Only, he had not looked as though he were playing.

Amid these jumping thoughts, some peace overtook her too. As she sat in her room, she had at least a plan. Tell the truth in the presence of Lady Ernestine, who would be shocked, but might also understand that obeying Miss Sophy was something to do with it. At least then they might understand, these people who had shown such friendship to her. She would relax at last until the Horescombes came home. She would accept food and shelter and no more from them, despite what the princess may wish to give her. At least they would not believe her a thief at the last.

The princess was at Madame Godot's when she met Lady Staines, who could be spotted at any rate at a mile's distance, so strange was her sense of colour. Today she sported a shocking pink muslin, with *orange* ribbons, and a turquoise pelisse. Her ladyship had been one of the sources of *on dits* about Sophy Ludgate, and Emmeline desired to expand her knowledge a little, in view of their predicament.

'Your ladyship,' the princess said, 'what an arresting bonnet.' It was orange, like the ribbons, and was embellished by folds of purple grosgrain ribbon. She saw the small figure of Madame Godot cast her eyes in the air and tried not to laugh.

'From someone of your taste, Your Highness,' said her ladyship smugly, 'I am complimented highly.'

Emmeline thought that "arresting" was not quite an admission of admiration, but smiled brightly.

'Is Staines in town?'

Her ladyship's face expressed a little distaste.

'Thankfully, my son does not accompany me.' She laughed, and the princess joined her. 'I love my son dearly, but it is no use denying he is a prig, set to spoil my amusements.'

'He is not yet married?'

'No, though I hope he may do soon. And whoever she is, I hope she leads him a merry dance. Really, I am a most *unnatural* mother.'

Emmeline liked Lady Staines, and agreed that her son, whom she had not seen in three years, was the biggest prig imaginable. 'Perhaps, with that young girl whom you told me of, Miss Sophy Ludgate wasn't it, due to be presented, you might have your wish.'

'Oh, what a treat that would be to watch, from the distance of the Dower House at least. She might drive him distracted in a very short time. And he *might* just offer for her as she's an heiress, and the ward of an earl. He is tremendously focussed on improving his estates and standing in the world. Whatever her reputation, he is just self-satisfied enough to believe he could tame her.'

'I admit that I have long wanted to know her full story, for I am, you know, tiresomely inquisitive.'

'But not a gossip, I know,' said Lady Staines. 'Of course I would not wish to bandy tales with a young girl's reputation at stake, like the foul Viscountess Swanson.'

'I shall never divulge a word!' said Emmeline seriously.

'Well,' said her ladyship, dropping her voice and

leaning in confidentially, 'perhaps we may adjourn to a coffee house nearby so as to discuss it?'

The ladies did so.

'Well, there is no doubting that the young lady sails close to the wind. Lady Ernestine was rather too lenient, I think, and allowed her to go out with her maid shopping or walking in the park. And of course, that allowed her to have encounters with who knows who. And then, you know, since she was not out, she was allowed no balls — but she was permitted to go with her particular friends to musical evenings, and small parties where there was dancing. That was quite enough to get a young girl as fascinating as she into trouble.'

The princess frowned. This seemed serious.

'Oh, nothing risqué, as old Viscountess Swanson has set about, saying she should be denied vouchers to Almacks.'

'Oh, dear!'

'Oh with the earl and Lady Ernestine as her sponsors, there is little fear of that. Maria Sefton is one of Ernestine's best friends.'

Lady Sefton was a patroness of Almacks, that elite ballroom, which every young lady desired to go to and where many had met their match.

'Then what *does* her reputation suggest?'

'Oh, that she is headstrong. A visit to the opera when she had been forbidden. The enticing of the recluse Mr Forster out of seclusion. Apparently she persuaded him she had talent on the pianoforte, which she does not.' Emmeline laughed, think that she might have done such things herself only a few years ago. 'Persuading young Lamb to supply the carriage for the opera evening, which his mama was highly displeased about. And then there was a visit to Astley's Amphitheatre, which is not certain, but Viscountess Swanson has set it about that she saw her there, accompanied by Miss Oakshott. It is rumoured that Sir Hugh Symington had arranged the visit, for it was his carriage the girls entered.'

'I expect she wished to see the equestriennes.'

'Indeed. But Lady Ernestine patently did not want her to do so yet. And she went anyway. She has never, you know, been seen in a gentleman's company alone. Which just about preserves her reputation. But it is quite clear that she does as she pleases.' Her ladyship paused, with her cup half raised to her mouth. 'Oh, you have inspired me Your Highness! I *must* introduce the new heiress to my son at the first opportunity...'

Emmeline laughed and soon took her leave.

As she rode back to Grosvenor Square she thought of Beth. Nothing about the Sophy she knew seemed like the description. Perhaps she was led astray by some other young lady, and then, of course, her sweetness guaranteed that any young cub she met must be willing to do anything for her. It all seemed to Emmeline like childhood desires, to see the play or the famous horsewomen, or to play a trick on some reserved gentleman for amusement.

Beth was showing more vivacity the more she relaxed, but somehow this wilfulness described did not mesh with her personality. But the princess knew that many a story got embellished in the retelling, and Beth could be the victim of some silly mistakes and some bad luck. The Vauxhall incident seemed the worst of all, as the most dangerous. But it appeared that it was not well-known, for Lady Staines did not mention it. That was good. Emmeline found herself solicitous for Beth's — or Sophy's reputation.

Chapter 9

Life at the marquis's house took on a rather different aspect the next morning. Dow was gone, and George was acting butler. Again, he looked his gratitude at Beth, but they did not talk of it. In his dark, unadorned livery, he looked very handsome and Beth smiled at him shyly, which butler-like, he did not see. Frost, the under-butler, did not evince any jealousy that Beth could see, and the marquis told her that he had agreed to continue working under George for the trial period, with an option to seek preferment at another house, with a good character provided.

Beth relaxed a great deal. It seemed her accent, so honed by Miss Sophy for her own devices, did not let her down. Indeed, it seemed more natural to her now than her own. She had already softened her country burr since she'd been at Lady Foster's, after all. She was, she thought, a natural mimic.

She displayed this as she was called to the princess's room the next morning, wearing her pelisse ready for the ride they had decided on at dinner the previous evening. The French maid was putting the princess's hair back and fussing around as she dressed her mistress in a handsomely frogged riding dress and set a pretty tricorne hat atop, an ironic reference to another time. The maid pulled the net over the princess's face, and her mistress said, 'The puce muslin today, Cécile,' which caused the maid to explode into a volley of words.

When Cécile left in another minute or two, Beth could not help ape her response, flinging her hands in the air in Gallic excitement, 'But no, Yourrr 'ighneess, you must *nev-err* wear puce, it drains the skin *entirelee!*' She ended with the maid's gesture in the air.

The princess laughed, saying, 'You might be in the theatre, my dear Beth!' and Beth, glad to be called by her name again, had to admit it was still a possibility. Though for the sake of her honour, she hoped not.

They rode together in the early morning, and by arrangement did not stop to greet friends, the marquis quite seeing the problem, as Emmi phrased it, of the introduction. Once on the ride, Beth was startled to see Miss Oakshott, friend of Miss Sophy, but that young lady was too busy regarding Her Highness's pelisse, so obviously a Paris creation. Beth grew to relax on the ride, glad to have a horse beneath her again as she had had on the farm, but not since. Certainly, it had never been such a fine beast, but she had learnt to ride early and was a natural, though the side-saddle was an adjustment.

'Does not Miss Fox have a fine seat, Wrexham?' the princess asked with mischief.

He looked over at Beth and smiled. 'Very admirable. Though I thought to begin with that it was some time since you've ridden, Miss Fox.'

'It is, rather, my lord.'

'Wrexham.' He replied. 'We discussed this.'

The princess's eyebrows flew up. This was not an honour bestowed on every young lady of their acquaintance.

'Very well, my lord — I mean Wrexham.' Beth smiled a little. 'But you promised not to bully me if I did call you so.' She was surprised to hear herself tease him, rather as though he were a footman at the Hall.

'And I shall be Emmeline,' said the princess, taking in their smiles. 'You have no idea how my title chafes at me. I am determined to marry soon, if only so I might drop it entirely.'

'That seems a little *extreme*,' said Beth, seriously. There was a beat, then, caught by the ridiculousness of this, they all laughed.

When they returned to the house, they breakfasted together and the chatter followed smoothly, Emmeline bearing more than her equal share in the nonsense. 'I see that you do not wish to gad about with me, my dear Beth, but what on earth are you to do with yourself all day?'

'I believe Miss Fox is a great reader, Emmi.'

The princess looked at Beth, clearly disappointed. '*Really?* I admit I read none but the most fashionable books, and even then only the pages my friends mark for me. I must be alone in finding *Glenarvon* quite tedious.'

'I have not read it,' said Beth.

'I'm afraid it would mean nothing to you if you have not been much in the *ton.* The writer gives new names to some notables and makes them either ridiculous or villains in her plot,' said the marquis, disapprovingly.

'You've *read* it then?' said Beth rather cheekily and he laughed again. 'Should I like it as a tale alone?' she asked, sipping her chocolate.

'I believe it has little merit if one is not scandalised by the gossip,' he replied.

'But you cannot stay and read *all* day, you will be most thoroughly bored,' said Emmeline, bringing the point around.

'Well, I might walk with Aggie in the square.'

'Who, pray, is Aggie?'

'A chambermaid,' said the marquis, as though shocked at the princess's ignorance.

Beth raised her eyebrows at him.

'Well, if you are going to walk with a maid, you may as well walk with me,' said Emmeline, noting the teasing, but ignoring it. 'I can put off some of my engagements.'

'Pray do not. And if I were to walk with you, we would be accosted at every turn.'

The princess sighed and said breezily, 'I *am*

frightfully fashionable.' Beth grinned at her. If only she could see them as her friends from the Hall, or her own jesting family, she could relax. Actually, the teasing tone between the brother and sister was quite inviting.

'I shall supply her with books, have no fear,' said the marquis, attacking his ham.

'And will you be at home? I should not leave her here if you *are*...'

'*Aggie* shall accompany her in the library,' said the marquis primly, highlighting the name, which made Beth look at him, quelling his teasing. 'All the proprieties shall be met.' The marquis turned to Beth. 'Does Aggie read? Must I supply her with books too in contrition for forgetting her name?'

She frowned him down as though he were but a footman at the board in the Hall. 'I do not know if she reads, but it would certainly be kind if you did.'

'Well I suppose there are some picture books somewhere if she does not know her letters.'

'If she does not read she will have work to get on with, no doubt.'

'Stitching? Poor work. You have convinced me that my staff should do nothing but read. I shall see to their education.' He said this in the same teasing tone and was shocked to encounter one of Beth's sharp looks.

'Education is not the subject of jests. It might amaze you how much your servants would appreciate it.'

The princess broke in. 'But how then would our furniture be polished or our dinners be cooked?' she said, with a laugh. Since Beth had begun to drop her guard with her hosts, her face displayed her displeasure at this.

To appease her, the marquis said, smiling in her direction, 'I'm sure many servants might be capable of both.'

'What are you two about?' said Emmeline, pouting. 'You seem to have jests I have no notion of.'

'It is only that I was forward enough to reveal my shock that the marquis does not know the names of his own household.'

'Well, what about it?' said Emmeline, smiling at the footman who served her a roll. 'I daresay he has a hundred servants in his houses, and so very many leave, you know.'

'Not Aggie. She has been here for a full four years, though she has been above stairs only in the last year.'

'You are a very strange girl. How can you know so much about a *servant* in but two days?'

Beth was too annoyed to avoid answering, 'By *asking* her!'

'If that surprises you Emmi, you would be shocked at the subject of our meeting last night,' Wrexham said, amused.

'Yes. Neither of you have told me what occurred, beyond the good news that Beth is staying until the Horescombes return.'

'Well —' the marquis caught Beth's eyes again,

Beth and the Mistaken Identity

and nodded the servants from the room. 'Beth has organised my entire household. I have dismissed the butler, and promoted a footman.'

'Dow gone? Well, I can't say I liked him, though I was never sure why. Rather more — oily than Wright. And a footman in his place? But isn't there Frost, the under-butler?'

The marquis glanced at Beth. 'You must be pleased to know that my sister remembers *some* of our servants' names.' The he turned back to his sister. 'Miss Fox feels that Frost might have been infected by Dow's ways, and suggested George.'

'*Infected — George*?' said Emmeline, looking from one to the other, then settling on Beth. 'What on earth can you know about George?'

Beth was at a loss to construct an answer, but the marquis answered wickedly, 'she met him at midnight in the library!'

'Beth!' shrieked Emmeline, the duenna.

Beth looked repressively at the marquis and answered. 'Your brother is being deliberately provocative. It is only that I went to the library for a book on the first evening, and George the footman entered the library afterwards.'

'She caught him stealing the brandy! And then she got him to tell her about the upset in the household since Wright retired.'

'Dear Wright!' Then the princess focused, 'Stealing the …? And you reward him with promotion?'

'Miss Fox will explain.'

'No, no! I prefer to remain in ignorance,' said the

princess unexpectedly. 'Let me tell you instead about my proposed meeting with Annabel Moreley! It is the biggest scandal of the season…'

After breakfast, on their way to their rooms to freshen up, the princess caught Beth's arm, and leaned into her confidingly.

'Forget what I said to you about going too far, my dear. I now see that you are the perfect wife for Wrexham. See how you make him laugh?' Beth made a sound of protest. 'I feared you too young before, but now I see you will be able to manage the household admirably. Do not get too close to the servants, however, my dear. Over-familiarity leads to laxity, my mama told me.'

There was so much in this little speech to object to, so much to be embarrassed by, so much to correct, that Beth hardly knew where to start. 'Your brother reminds me of mine, he cannot pass an opportunity to tease.'

'You have a brother, then? Might I know him?'

Beth, startled at giving more away than she meant, could not help laughing at this. 'No, he is a little younger than me, and remains in the country.'

'I hope I shall meet him one day, dear Beth.'

Beth smiled at her, rather sadly. 'I do not think you ever will.'

Wrexham was at his club when his friend, the Earl of Grandiston joined him, and they settled down to a game of cards *à deux*. The earl was as elegant as ever, and beyond making a disparaging remark on Wrexham's shirt points (not as stiff as his lordship's standards demanded) he opted to forgo talking to play cards.

'You seem a little *distrait*, Wrexham, not your usual gregarious self.'

Wrexham gave this sally a twisted smile. Gregarious could never describe him. 'I have a problem.'

'I am ever at your disposal, but I thought your fortune more intact than most.'

The marquis gave the joke another smile. 'It is a problem of another sort at all.'

'Ah, a woman!'

Wrexham raised his brows. 'How did you guess?'

The earl dealt the cards and said dryly, 'There are only two sorts of problems in this world, Wrexham. Money and women.'

'Well, *you* cannot help me my friend. You are too happy with your beautiful countess to understand me. How is Lady Grandiston, by the way?'

'Oriana is blooming. Our second child is due any day. I would not have left her, but she had her particular friends to visit and they wished to discuss me, so I was ejected from my own home.'

Wrexham discarded two cards and said, 'Your second child! You are blessed.'

'I am.' Grandiston met his eyes, 'but there is always the fear—' Wrexham looked his sympathy. 'But I am come to my club for distraction. So tell me what your problem with women is. You should be married by now, anyway.'

'All men who are married seek to rob me of my bachelorhood, I find.'

Grandiston grinned. 'You avoid the subject. If you think you cannot confide in me, Toby, I shall question our friendship.'

'Some of it I cannot disclose, as affecting not my honour, but that of another.'

'Oh don't tell me Emmi is in hot water again after being so new to town. That girl was always the most outrageous young minx...'

'No, it is not Emmi. And you shouldn't speak thus of your social superiors.'

Grandiston grinned again. 'Apologise to Her Highness for me. I jumped to conclusions, based on previous experience.'

'Are you referring to the gossip about my sister's adventures? Simply old wives' chatterings.'

'Remember it was me who helped you push her through her room window before your mother realised she was not abed, the night of the Faversham's Masked Ball.'

'What a girl she was. But she is a sober princess these days.'

'I doubt it. You are still avoiding the question. What troubles you? Let me guess: some tall, blond, cool beauty has you in her toils.'

'No. But why should you think that?'

'Do you not know that that is your type? I have seen you with countless women fitting that description in these last five years.' He raised one eyebrow. 'And do not think that your excessive admiration of my Oriana has gone unnoticed.'

'I would have lain my heart at her feet if she would have had me. But unaccountably she preferred you.'

Grandiston smiled smugly. 'Yes she did. So what is your problem?'

'A little dab of a girl, whom Emmi is helping—'

'Yes?' encouraged Grandiston, when he paused.

'She does not *fawn* at me. That is the first thing. She is not shy of me, not in the way I am used to —' he paused. 'I am aware that I sound like a coxcomb. But *you* know, Grandiston.'

'Yes, shy and afraid of your glamour, or pushing and flirting. I remember being an eligible *parti*. It could get quite exhausting.'

'She is shy, but about the *position* she is in — which I cannot enlighten you about — not about any awareness of me as an eligible man. And she tells me off when she thinks I behave badly, and then is embarrassed that she has opened her mouth.' He laid down his cards. 'I cannot say why I find that so enticing. And then, she looks sometimes like a little wren with a broken wing, and I feel I need to — to —' Wrexham was stunned that he'd talked so much, and met Grandiston's eye. 'I have only known her a scant three days, and I must be careful not to raise expectations I cannot meet.'

'That is not everything you should be careful

about,' said Grandiston. Watching him.

'But she seems not to have any expectations, else she would not challenge me as she does. She does not flatter me, and I find it so refreshing. She is young, but somehow not...'

Grandiston shook his head, laughing. 'I fear, my friend, that you are too far gone for any help I might offer.'

Beth had decided to enjoy her last days as a lady. Things could not, after all, get much worse. The brother and sister would be very angry with her, no doubt, and perhaps really seek her punishment, but that was not today. For these days she could be a friend, and perhaps a help, to both. Beth, sitting with some embroidery that the princess had discarded automatically setting stitches, watching her dress for dinner.

'I am meant to be embroidering those handkerchiefs for Toby, but somehow or other, I never seem to finish. It is his birthday next week, and it is just a token.' She looked at herself in the mirror. 'This new silk looks pretty, does it not?'

'It is ravishing,' said Beth regarding the russet silk, almost dark orange in colour that went so well with Emmeline's rich brown hair.

The princess turned to her, 'Oh Beth, do let me give you a dress to wear this evening.'

'You know I will not,' smiled Beth. 'You have tried to buy and lend me clothes since I got here.

And we would miss dinner if I agreed. How could we take up a dress of yours in but an hour? I am some inches shorter, you know.'

'Oh, Cécile could do it!'

'I assure you, she could not. I am an experienced needlewoman myself and to take up one of your silks or even a muslin, without completely destroying it, would take much more than an hour.'

'How *do* you know these things?'

'Why, I have made dresses for years.'

'Sweet!' said the princess, touching her cheek. 'You can hardly have done *anything* for years.'

But she could. 'I do not need to change.'

'But only two dresses for a week. How will you bear it?'

Beth only laughed.

Emmeline suddenly put down the gloves she had begun to put on. 'I shall leave off even black gloves tonight. I think it time.'

There was a brittleness in Emmeline's voice that called Beth to say, 'You are very young to be a widow.'

'Yes,' said Emmeline, and Beth heard a crack in her voice.

'You must be so very distressed, I'm sorry to raise the sad subject.'

The princess sat on the gold brocade sofa beside her, with a rustle of silk. 'I can say this to you, Beth — and to no other. I am *not* distressed at all.'

Beth stopped sewing and took Emmi's hands. 'Were you very unhappy?'

'I could not believe that someone so handsome, so charming at first, could be so *cruel*.' She closed her eyes as Beth grasped her hands more strongly. 'Cécile knows, of course. She bathed my wounds, she was my only confidante. You must *never* tell Wrexham, Sophy, he would be so hurt that he could not help me.'

'Oh, Emmi!' said Beth, tears coursing down her face. The princess released one hand and touched Beth's tears wonderingly.

'I was never allowed these. One had to show face, you know.'

'Yes,' said Beth, pityingly.

'It was not really so bad. He was gone a great deal, and then he fell off that horse.' She hung her head. 'I am ashamed of what I felt then. It was not gladness, but it was — *relief*.'

'My mother used to say that you feel what you feel, there is no shame in any of it. It is only what you *do* that matters.'

'She sounds very wise. Maybe that is what makes me trust you, Beth. That something about you that comes from having wise parents.'

'Perhaps you should not trust me. And only one of my parents was wise. My father was far from wise,' Beth's eyes moved like the princess's before her, to the past. There he was again, drunk and demanding, or crying and begging forgiveness.

The princess stood, saying, 'I'm so glad Wrexham found you, my dear. So very glad. Let us do something with your hair at least before dinner.'

'Yes, Your Highness.'

The princess hugged her and said, looking at the discarded sewing. 'You will be sure to finish them before you go, dear Beth, will you not?'

And Beth said, 'To be sure I will.' And was rewarded not by the polite nod or small smile that would have been given to a maid, but by a hug and a kiss from a friend.

Sophy Ludgate did not think that house parties could be any duller. She was exiled here as penance for the tiniest of crimes, really. She had merely slipped from the London house by the kitchen entrance, taking a maid, of course (so what the fuss was about, she could hardly fathom), to do a little shopping in town and perhaps meet some friends in the park at the walking hour. Before she had done more than reach the park, she had been rudely accosted by the passengers in an ancient landau, bearing the Earl of Horescombe's crest.

Miss Wilhelmina cried faintly, while Lady Ernestine read her a lecture. They were met on their return to Horescombe House by the calm figure of Miss Florencia in the hall, her harsh face set, hands clasped before her on her shabby gown. How she could give herself the airs of a duchess wearing the same had Sophy baffled. Yet somehow she did. Sophy was uncaring of Lady Ernestine's frank lecture, and only a little less so of Miss Wilhelmina's tears, but still she shook somewhat at shabby Miss Florencia.

'The general requests that you have your maid pack for a house party, Sophy. We leave in one hour.'

'Where —?'

But Miss Florencia Fosdyke had walked away.

'Are we to go too, Florencia?' asked her sister, running rather excitedly behind her. 'But we have nothing to wear to such a —' The sisters disappeared into the Green Salon.

Lady Ernestine sighed, but as Sophy looked on, her face had changed suddenly, to a look of mischief.

And now Sophy knew why. The general had accepted (belatedly, and solely due to Sophy's need to be taught a lesson, no doubt) an invitation to a house party in the Devon home of an old war compatriot, Colonel Asquith. And by dint of donating some evening dresses to the Misses Fosdykes, Lady Ernestine had been able to forgo the trip entirely in favour of a visit of her own, thus avoiding the dullest set of guests that it could be possible to assemble. All of them were ancient, over forty at least, and Sophy was regretting her London escapade with every sentiment Lady Ernestine could wish. All day Miss Wilhelmina and the ladies chatted and embroidered, while the men took out their guns in the park, and the only possible companion on Sophy's walks was Miss Fosdyke herself. She was not a chatterbox, and Sophy felt her spirits drop a little — not a state she usually indulged in.

Miss Florencia broke her silence one day to say, 'I know that you believe we do these things to punish you, Sophia, but I assure you that is not so.'

Sophy stopped walking then, and her companion joined her, hardly heeding the magnificent, turbulent sea view from the cliff walk, or the wind that whipped at their bonnets. 'Oh no? And was that not a smile of victory that I saw on Lady Ernestine's face when she saw us off?'

A little muscle moved at the side of Miss Fosdyke's mouth, softening her harsh face for a moment. 'Perhaps. But it is you who turn obedience into a game of chess, Sophy. You know it is so.'

'Perhaps.' She exchanged the most understanding look she had ever had with Miss Fosdyke. She walked on.

'So why do you do so? You must know that the restrictions laid upon you were for your own protection?' said her elder, marching at her side.

'So everyone tells me. But to me it is the desire of the world to — to strangle me.'

Miss Fosdyke got out a noise that could have been a snort. They walked on for a mile before she spoke again. 'Do you not think that there is danger in this world? Even a *shade* on a lady's reputation makes her unable to wed a respectable man. Lady Ernestine's desire, all our desires, are simply to help you avoid consequences that you cannot, in your inexperience, understand.'

'But I do understand the consequences. Why do you think I always arrange to be chaperoned?'

'You did not think of the *consequences* for your maid. Seven years in service, Sophia, and now she is cast off without a character.'

The words were harsh, but Miss Fosdyke's tone less so. Sophy felt a stab of real guilt. She believed that Beth, whose hands could sew and dress hair like an angel, would find another position quickly. Surely her skills counted for something? She would not be drawn into their tale of dire consequences. People had sought to do so all her life just to stop her doing what she wished. To stop her doing *anything*, it seemed to her. When she came into her own fortune, or when she married, she would seek Beth out and take her back. She was not so ungrateful as they all thought. Of course, that may be some years, but that was not her fault.

They continued to walk silently, their little piece of connection lost.

The evenings were as dull as the days. A lot of people, some very old indeed, told stories around the dinner table that did not interest her, and an old roué flirted with her, and the Misses Fosdyke played the pianoforte (rather better than she feared, but such sad tunes). She could not help it, she was planning an escape. Of course, she would go back to London, and to Horescombe House eventually, but Lady Ernestine and the general deserved to worry. She looked over at Miss Wilhelmina, very nearly pretty in Lady Ernestine's fine but simple navy silk, which became her willowy figure. Her pale brown hair was knotted becomingly, which had made her sister sniff, and her usually anxious face was animated by a sparkle of joy resulting from the nonsense of the indiscriminate old roué. This, thought Sophy sadly, might be the apex of that lady's social adventures. Well, she was sorry, and she might have to leave a note to assuage Miss Wilhelmina's feelings, but she was already quite far along with her plan. That she had to enlist a maid and tell some untruths did not stop her, the Misses Fosdyke could explain that it was not the girl's fault.

Being caught by Lord Horescombe frightened her a little. His saddened looks had alternated with sharp ones, when she had been slow to join in the dull dinner conversation. He had caught her up in the hall after the first dinner and said in a low voice, 'Sophy, you will be your sparkling best at breakfast tomorrow. I now remember why I refused all such invitations from Asquith for the last years, for a very tiresome set of people he knows. But as I am here *solely* because you cannot be trusted in town, let us hope this will mend your ways in that regard. You will be more than civil, Sophy.' She cast down her eyes demurely, but he was not deceived, but continued threateningly. 'I have lived a long life, and I have many such acquaintances to visit, some even *duller*. It makes little odds to me. As long as I have dinner, a horse to ride and a library to escape to, I shall do. But will *you*?' He'd held up her chin. 'I like you, Sophy, you have something of your mother's spirit. But disobedience in the ranks is what I have never stood for, and never will!'

Well, Sophy liked him too. And Lady Ernestine and her bookish ways. And even the Misses Fosdyke. Miss Wilhelmina had come into her room after dinner one night and said, 'Oh Sophy, I do hope you are enjoying yourself as much as I am!' Sophy merely gaped. 'The company is most elevated and charming, and my room has a view of the sea. And only imagine, our host has caused a fire to be lit there. Such a waste, only for me, but so very welcome. And wearing Lady Ernestine's dress, which I know I will return to her, but it is so lovely and I only had to have it pinned a trifle, with silk pins, you know, so fine that they will not mark it I'm sure. And I have another *three* on loan. Florencia has the same number, but finds only the grey silk plain enough for her, and chafes at the ribbons, but she looks almost a girl again. I mean to encourage her to try the wine silk too, before we leave, for I remember her in a muslin of the same colour when we were younger, and it became her so well. Oh Sophy, I know that you would rather be in London, and I did so long to see more of the city myself, but it is the happiest chance that we get to come here, too. Do you not think so, my dear girl?' She added the last anxiously, and Sophy determined, in a heroic spirit, to delay her running-off until Miss Wilhelmina had a few more days of her visit. She patted her hand, therefore, and said, 'I'm so glad you are enjoying it, ma'am. I believe I never saw you look prettier than tonight!' causing her chaperone to blush. She could not put off her plan longer, or it would not teach Lady Ernestine (now visiting more amusing friends in Kent) a lesson. When they saw how determined she was, the Horescombes could not, and would not, send her to another party such as this.

The result was that some days later than she had planned, and only two days before the party was set to break up properly, Sophy, wearing the maid Betty's Sunday best dress, cloak and bonnet (in exchange for a heavenly pink muslin and real wool pelisse which Betty would hide for the moment), stole from the house and met Bill, a carter, and brother of Betty. 'Quick!' she said to this rather startled young man, 'We shall be seen!'

Automatically, Bill held out his hand, and pulled her up, while his sister whispered instructions to him. With her small carpet bag (also belonging to Betty), and her legs swinging on the back of the cart, Sophy felt herself to be in heaven, unfettered by other wills than her own. She joined the stagecoach at Bixford, for the first time in her life *really* without chaperone, and found that she was too fascinated by a cast of characters it would never normally fall upon her to meet, to be at all afraid.

She had left a note for Miss Wilhelmina, apologising and assuring her that she was not in danger, but had only taken the stage to London. It would not matter, the house would not rise for hours, and they could never catch it. By that time she would be in London and she meant to — but here she hit a bump. She had thought of little but escape. Little except showing them all that she would not be tamed. Normally, she had a perfectly obvious (to her) end in view. A visit to a play, or to some attraction she was forbidden, a meeting with someone exciting. But this venture was simply a check-mate to Lady Ernestine, with no other end in view. She worried for a trifle. Was this silly? Then she looked at the cadaverous figure of the lawyer, opposite, who said such happy things in a miserable voice, 'Lovely day, what?' and knew she would not have missed this for the world. There was a farmer, complaining in almost indecipherable Devon dialect about his absent landowner, a lady who snored and scratched at herself in a most diverting way while sleeping, plus two boys of about fourteen who insisted on playing cards, though the bumps of the road sent them scattering every two minutes, the boys pushing at her legs and arms to retrieve them. She felt alive and glad, whatever the resulting punishment. If they sent her to Scotland, even, Sophy would find a way to escape. To be ruled was never to be her fate!

She had it! She would return to the London house and take a high hand with the servants. She had at least a day's grace, she thought. And she could change, and take a maid to the park, and when she returned to London herself, Lady Ernestine would admit that they should talk. It was a small victory, perhaps, and that irked her.

But this plan was not to be put into action. For when she stepped from the stage, Sophy found a much larger adventure awaited her.

On her way down to dinner that night, Beth pulled George aside. 'George…'

'Dobson, miss'

'What? Oh yes, I'm sorry Dobson. But you must mention the picture frames to the housekeeper. It still is not done.'

Dobson drew himself up to his full height, 'I shall discuss the matter with her this evening, miss.'

'Not yourself, I hope,' said Beth, in an urgent under-breath. 'It would be wiser to tell a footman to say that *his lordship* had mentioned the picture frames, else you will be the housekeeper's bounden enemy.'

Dobson looked at her quizzically, 'Yes, miss. Is there anything else, miss?'

'Oh, many things. The flowers are beginning to wilt, and the furniture on the first floor landing has dust beneath. But best not mention it. Hopefully she'll be so humiliated at having the picture frames mentioned that she will take charge as she should.'

'Yes miss,' said Dobson, looking after her as she bustled off after the princess.

The marquis had been making his languid way downstairs for dinner and had observed his house guest, still wearing her rose sprigged muslin, in deep conversation with his new butler. As Beth disappeared into the dining room, he approached Dobson. 'What was Miss Fox discussing with you - eh - Dobson?'

The butler looked suitably inscrutable. 'She was discussing some housekeeping deficiencies, my lord.'

'Housekeeping—?' the marquis looked around the hall for evidence.

'Not so obvious, my lord,' said the butler. 'Dust on picture frames on the first floor, sir.'

The marquis looked fascinated. 'Is that all?'

'Dust under furniture, your lordship.' The marquis looked below the console table opposite him, shocked, but the butler cast his eyes above. 'And she has drawn my attention to the flowers, my lord.' Dobson's eyes moved to the hall arrangement of tall lilies in a handsome Chinese vase. The marquis's eyes followed.

'They look well enough ...' said the marquis, then moved forward, despite himself. 'No! They *are* a little sad. Have them replaced.'

The butler gave the cough that all butlers used to forewarn of a view of their own, 'Might it be tomorrow, my lord?'

The marquis raised his brows.

'It is just that Miss Fox has advised me that it may be better, to re-establish smooth running of the house, that I have just *one* thing mentioned to Mrs Fitch, in the hopes that this hint will spark improvement elsewhere.' The marquis seemed to be considering. 'Upon reflection, my lord, I cannot but think that Miss Fox might be wise.'

The marquis nodded. 'War at the offset, eh, Dobson? Yes, you might want to avoid that. Perhaps you should get someone else to mention it to Mrs Fitch. And say it comes from me.'

'Miss Fox has already advised me to do so, my lord.'

The marquis went into dinner. 'It seems,' he announced as he sat down, 'that our housekeeping does not come up to scratch, Emmi.' Beth blushed, wanting a hole to open up and swallow her.

'Really? *I* hadn't noticed,' said Emmeline, indicating at the maid who was dispensing the soup from a handsome tureen.

'That doesn't surprise me. Princesses never see what their chattels do,' answered the marquis to his sister, but regarding Beth's embarrassment with amusement. 'It is the third time I have been put right in the running of the household by Miss Fox.'

'I am sorry, my lord; it was none of my business.'

'Well, I think you very clever to be so knowledgeable, Beth,' said the princess, comfortingly. 'I know you are only teasing, Tobias, but you are distressing our friend. Please desist.'

'Certainly, Your Highness,' her brother said, mockingly inclining his head. 'I'm sorry, Miss Fox. And I assure you I *am* very grateful.'

'I know you must think it a dreadful intrusion, my lord. It is just that, as Geor — Dobson has only just begun to run the house, it seemed to me that he should begin aright,' she had dropped her voice to avoid being overheard by the footmen, 'And I cannot help noticing when things are not just as they ought to be.'

'I expect it was your mother that taught you,' said the princess, 'Beth has the wisest mother, Wrexham. No, don't look like that, Tobias, she did not tell me her name, only of her wisdom.'

Beth tried to turn the subject again, anxious that the marquis should understand. 'It was not my mother, actually, but a housekeeper in a house I — lived in.' This was not precisely a lie. She wished them to remember later, that but for her name, she had never told them a lie. 'But I should not have interfered. I beg your pardon.'

'And so you should. It is not often that young guests order my household to their liking.' He laughed at her, then. 'Oh, do not look so, pray, my dear. I am very grateful to you for doing so quickly what I might have done some months ago, if I had noticed ...'

'There is not much to notice. And gentlemen do not concern themselves with such things ...'

'You are a marvel, Beth! You have scarce been here three days and yet you have proved yourself so useful already.'

'Useful to you, Emmi?' laughed Wrexham, 'What concern do you have in the running of the household as long as your dinner arrives in time?'

'Why none at all, Wrexham. It is just that I have been able to talk of so many things to Beth. Lady's concerns, you know,' she added when it seemed as though he guessed a little too much. Then her eyes sparkled mischievously, 'It is almost as though I had a sister.'

Beth's face froze and it was some time before she could look up from her soup again. By that time, the marquis was chatting to his sister about a new *on dit*, involving the bets in the gentleman's clubs on the pretenders to the newest heiress in town, the beautiful Miss Delphine Delacroix. 'The main money is on Gascoigne.'

'Dear Titus! He led me out for my first waltz. And then Mama forbade me to do so again. Only the country dances for the dangerous Viscount Gascoigne.'

'Yes, well, much as I care for Titus, there is no saying he's not in hot water with the duns. Mama was ambitious for you, and she feared Gascoigne's charm,' said the marquis comfortably.

'She was certainly ambitious,' said his sister coolly.

'And see how well it turned out.'

Beth could just reach Emmeline's hand beneath the table. 'Yes,' the princess said brightly. 'Just see!'

He picked up his own words and said, 'I'm sorry, Emmi. I should not refer to your loss.'

'Never mind, Wrexham. I'm a Brunswick, after all, and we soldier on.' She gave a last squeeze of Beth's hand and the marquis could see that they exchanged a look of tender intimacy. The conversation turned.

In due time, the marquis stayed with the port, while the ladies withdrew. He joined them rather sooner than was his wont in the drawing room, and surprised them in an embrace, his sister, his frivolous, guarded sister, sobbing on Beth's shoulder. Beth exchanged a sober glance with him above the princess's coiled hair, and he closed the door noisily.

Emmi straightened quickly, still with her back to him. 'I was just thanking Beth for joining us, Wrexham,' she said brightly, but he saw her handkerchief fly to her hidden face.

'I do not remember being given much of an option,' said Beth, teasing Emmi to lift her spirits.

'No indeed, we have been very ruthless, and have imprisoned you like one of Mrs Radcliffe's heroines.'

'Oh, yes. To be entombed in the finest house I have stayed in, with all my needs supplied is dreadful indeed!' laughed Beth. 'And I expect,' she added honestly, thinking of Miss Sophy in this situation, 'that if I'd *really* tried I *could* have escaped.'

The marquis was caught by something else. '*Is*

Beth and the Mistaken Identity

this the finest house you have ever stayed in, Miss Fox?'

Beth considered honestly, gazing around the large, high-ceiling drawing room, painted in delicate sea green, with the tallest of windows allowing in the light of the street-lamps, letting it fall over the Aubusson carpet. 'Well one was rather larger, being a country house,' she said, thinking of Foster Hall, 'and one, in London, was very ancient and strong, but I do think that this *is* the finest house.' She blushed, as the marquis smiled at her.

'I am very glad you approve,' he said.

The princess rose, and Beth rose too, but the marquis asked, 'Will you remain, Miss Fox? There is something I wish to discuss with you.'

'Well,' said Emmi, smoothing her skirts, 'I should not allow it, but if you leave the door open, I will. I find myself sleepier than usual tonight.'

'Some hot milk!' said Beth solicitously. Emmeline laughed, bent to kiss Beth's cheek, and left them together.

'Come with me to the library. This room has too much of an echo for private conversation.'

She went after him, her heart in her throat, afraid somehow to be alone with him.

She took a seat on the old leather sofa, which smelt faintly of the cologne of a long line of marquises, she thought, and he stood before the fire.

'I wanted to thank you, without the teasing, this time, for all your help with my household. I think it only a matter of time that the diversion from the course Dow had set us would have resulted in much discomfort for my sister and I. *And* a split in the household more difficult to address, without casting off the whole staff.' He said it easily, and it chilled Beth once more that people's lives could be so easily discarded. 'Ah, I have upset you again,' he looked sorry. 'Do not deny it, Miss Fox. I fear your face betrays your feelings very fully. Now what can I have said this time?'

'You talk of casting off people ... so easily,' she said, unable to stop herself.

'Did I? I spoke frivolously, I believe. I would not of course cast everyone off. You must realise that some of my people have been with the family for generations. They are in effect, under my protection, and I do not take this responsibility lightly, I assure you.' He smiled down at her, coming nearer. 'You are a strange little creature, Miss Fox. Making my house over in a way that someone your age might never even be aware of, and making a confidant of my sister, who does not, for all her rattling, confide easily.'

Beth's eyes raised to his, unable to look away.

'It is most unlike my sister to share her grief. I have tried, but our family has always been rather inept at sharing our feelings, or even showing them. That is why I am so very glad that Emmi has been able to share with you.' He turned, some feelings of his own overcoming him, and looked into the fire, one foot resting on the hearth. In the expression she read perhaps a little humiliation, a little envy of the princess's confidence, plus a deeper concern for her pain.

Beth was able to look at him without dissimulation then, when he could not see her. She admired his strong shoulders that she was beginning to understand bore so much. His hair curled at his high collar, his blue coat and buff *pantalons* were crafted to fit him perfectly — all the magnificence of the Marquis of Wrexham, just as she had seen him those few days ago. But now she knew his bearing sought to hide his burden under a show of casual relaxation, but she was not quite convinced. He was deeply concerned for his sister, and quite unable to help her, he believed.

'You are wrong you know.' His eyes turned towards her, laughing again, and she realised that marquises were not accustomed to being told they were wrong, especially by such very young ladies. But this was too important, she had seen his insecurity about his dealings with his sister and she must relieve him of this burden, if she could. 'You and your sister may not share your feelings conventionally, but you share all the same. You do so with humour and with teasing, and with all the affection of truly intimate family. How I envy you.' He looked struck. 'It means, you know, that when Emmi is able to share her — her grief, then all the doors will be open to her to do so. She does not fear you, Wrexham,' and for the first time she used his name naturally, 'and that is such an important thing.'

He came to her then, and sat nearer to her than was usual. He took her chin in one casual hand and her pulse raced. 'Who are you, small creature who has come into our lives and brought with you new happiness?'

She breathed and looked up at him, trembling beneath his fingers. 'I am someone who - who needs join your sister before she sleeps, my lord.'

He stood up, shaking his head, 'Of course. Goodnight, my dear Miss Fox.'

Chapter 10

Before George, or Dobson as she must now call him, had left on an errand of his master regarding the delicate and confidential matter of a carriage of burgundy sent from the coast, Beth had managed to talk with him. She supposed, when she heard his master gave him orders over breakfast, that this errand must be to do with the avoidance of the excise man, but no. It seemed the large haul was to be split among various gentleman's houses, and the marquis required the cart to be met, and the wine to be carefully packed into another carriage, to be sent off to his Kent estate. The butler's presence was necessary to oversee that the inn lads did not disturb the wine in the process, the marquis explained to Beth.

As Beth sat in her favourite chair in the library, reading, she feared she might be able to get used to this life. Often she felt the guilt of not being busy, and often found herself disposing articles more neatly around whatever room she was in, but the joy of reading for hours overcame it. Now she had the Iliad (thankfully in translation) and was engrossed in the tale of the Agamemnon and Achilles. 'Ach—ill—es,' she sounded to herself with a frown. Then light dawned and she said 'Achilles!' with the correct pronunciation. The marquis had stepped into the library at that moment and let out a short laugh, and Beth sat up abruptly.

'I came in to see what you had found to read today, before I go out. And I see you have entered the world of ancient Greece. I'm not sure my mama would have approved this reading for young ladies.'

'And you, my lord?'

'I have no objection.' He paused and thought a little, remembering some less salubrious passages, 'With some exceptions.' She smiled at him. 'You had never heard of Achilles?'

'Oh yes! My father had a dog so called, I just realised. It is merely that I had never seen the name written.'

He was smiling at her in that intimate, friendly way they had found together, and she returned it glowingly. 'Any other names that have caused you problems?'

'Almost all of them. I had to say Agamemnon aloud three times before I got it right. He is very unwise, of course, but now I believe it will be the name of my first child.'

'But what if it is a girl? I think that a very heavy chain to lay upon any infant.'

She smiled back, 'I am quite determined, Agamemnon it will be!'

'Enjoy your Trojan adventure, Miss Fox. I look forward to discussing it with you this evening.'

Beth settled down again with her book, until the princess stepped in on her way to a shopping appointment. She was wearing a luxurious ermine stole over her blue pelisse and the most enormous muff that Beth had ever seen.

'Oh darling Beth, I do hate to leave you with nothing to do but a dusty old book.'

'I am very content, I assure you,' said Beth equably. 'Emmi, do you know who Achilles is?' she asked as an afterthought, for she feared her ignorance had somehow shown her up.

'Someone Greek,' said Emmi.

'And Agamemnon?'

Emmi looked disgusted. 'Beth, if you continue in this vein, people will think you *bookish!*'

'I'm rather afraid I am.'

'Once your family returns and I show you around town, you will find other amusements. You are not much like your reputation, you know.'

'I fear it will not be so simple,' said Beth sadly.

'You will be in trouble, no doubt,' said the princess kindly. 'But I assure you the Horescombes will understand when I explain how wonderful you have been for us.' She bent and kissed her cheek briefly. 'Have fun with your fusty old book. I will be back in the afternoon.'

Alone, Beth swung her legs over the arms of

the chair, her head tucked into the side wing, and continued to read. She would not think about the Horescombes' return, she had vowed, but would enjoy the enchanting days left. An hour passed in perfect bliss.

The door to the library had remained ajar, and she saw Dobson's tall frame in the hall, and called him in, pulling herself upright once more.

'Dobson!'

As he entered, Beth was amused by his gravity of bearing, wearing his new responsibility well. He bowed, a fraction lower than her status as a young girl warranted. 'How can I help you, ma'am?'

Beth smiled. 'Excuse my inquisitiveness, Dobson, I merely wished to ask how Mrs Fitch took the criticism.'

A fraction of a smile crossed his face. 'Not well, Miss, and then again, very well indeed.' Beth's eyebrows raised. 'She was extremely put out miss, and was, I'm sorry to say, very harsh indeed on the upstairs maids. But I'm afraid two of them are newly arrived, miss, and did not quite know their duties. Not in full, I mean.'

'If they were not shown the correct way to go on, then it is not the girls' fault. It is Mrs Fitch's responsibility, after all, to see that the work is done to her standards. But she has been here some time? I find it very strange that the butler's behaviour alone can have had such an effect on her.'

'Yes, miss.' Dobson's face closed a little and he remained silent.

Beth and the Mistaken Identity

'Is there, perhaps, another reason?'

Dobson looked at her for a moment, then seemed to make a decision of trust. 'Well, miss, I do not think that Mrs Fitch would like it known, but she has developed a rheumatic complaint in the last two years that makes it difficult to climb stairs. She makes sure the ground floor is properly seen to, for she can manage one flight at the moment, but she no longer visits the upper floors. She made the effort yesterday, and suffered for it.'

Beth was sympathetic. 'How dreadful for her, she must fear to be turned off.'

'I believe so, ma'am, but the marquis is unusually kind to his dependants, and so I have told her.'

'I know. But it is dreadful to fear the loss of your home for so long,' she said with real feeling. She frowned. 'Tell me, is there another housemaid who is competent and has been here for a long time?'

'Meg, Miss. But I'm afraid that she is not a favourite of Mrs Fitch. If Meg instructs a newer maid and Mrs Fitch hears of it, well ...' George Dobson was surprised that he was jettisoning his disciplined discretion when talking to this young lady. There was no height in her manner at all, and he felt somehow safe to do so. Added to that, he knew she was the author of his unlooked-for promotion.

'Of course she is not a favourite. She is afraid, of course, that Meg — is it? — may steal her position.' Dobson looked down at her, fascinated. 'How old is Mrs Fitch?'

'Well, I hardly know, Miss. Perhaps sixty.'

'It is a hard life as a maid and housekeeper for all these years. And now rheumatism, which can make the best of people crotchety! Mrs Fitch needs some support, it is clear. But it must be done in a manner that makes her know that her position remains safe.' Beth had a thought. 'Was that a topic of the argument between Mrs Bates and her?'

'It was ma'am. Mrs Bates mentioned once that Mrs Fitch was derelict in her duties as a result of her sore bones, and Mrs Fitch took much offence.'

'That was cruel of Mrs Bates,' said Beth.

'I assure you ma'am, I believe it was the result of a difficult day for Cook. She was sorry almost the moment she spoke, but the damage was done. Then when Mrs Fitch disparaged her pastry, full war was engaged.'

Beth laughed. 'I think it would be.'

'Under Mr Wright, staff arguments were dealt with swiftly, and not allowed to fester. But Mr Dow would agree with one and then the other, and kept the fire burning.'

'Dreadful!' said Beth, imagining the damage to the entire household that such tensions between the upper servants could wreak.

'But miss, Cook is very skilled, and if the marquis was to hear ...' said Dobson, looking concerned.

'Don't fear. I shall discuss all this with the marquis, but I will tread lightly over the dispute. The main thing is to get Mrs Fitch some help, in a manner that does not terrify her.'

'I must go, miss, to meet the carriage.' Dobson bowed and walked to the door. Then, very much like George again, he turned to say, 'Thank you miss. It seems to me that you have already been the means for me to return the house to the days Mr Wright. If you can persuade the marquis to appoint an under-housekeeper, it will go a long way to helping.'

He left, but commanded another footman before departure, 'Have coals sent up for the library fire. Miss Fox is cold.'

Beth, wearing an 'old' shawl of Emmi's (the finest cashmere) did not feel cold at all, but appreciated the gesture very much.

Tobias Brunswick, Marquis of Wrexham, was on his way to his club to meet some cronies for an agreed game of cards, after he had performed more mundane tasks such as a drive through the park to exercise his horses and greet acquaintances. He tried to avoid the carriages containing young unmarried ladies and their mamas, but if old Lady Jobson had known him from birth, or Mrs Forest had been recently widowed, it was impossible to do so. He was introduced to their daughters, one shy and a little colourless, one much too loud, and was as charming as he could be, satisfying their mamas. He agreed to dance with both of them at upcoming engagements, and continued his park ride.

He plunged into deep thought, such that he missed the hail of several friends, on foot and on horseback, which he would be roasted for at a later date. He could not but compare the two young girls he had met to Miss Fox. He remembered finding her in the library yesterday, her feet over the arm of the chair, slightly swinging. Her fingers were thoughtlessly twirling one side ringlet, and she was raptly reading. He had stood watching that little face, which was pretty enough even when you could not see her fabulous eyes, and the soft brown of her hair. He was growing to love the slim blue gown she alternated with the other simple muslin. He saw an errant ankle beneath her hem, and something, that had been merely admiring and wondering at her effect on him, lit into a fire.

An ankle, he thought disgusted, had him shaking so much that he had not been able to go into the room lest he — *what*?

He did not really understand himself. Apart from the girls he had just met, there were many eligible ladies of great beauty in the *ton* that had somehow failed to light that fire. Some married ladies of high rank had lit it somewhat, and they had taken their pleasure together, but this was a new feeling to him. The fire was bound up in the quickness with which they had become friends, even though she was so terrified at first that he had thought she might shudder herself to death.

Beth and the Mistaken Identity

That terror, he thought now, had somehow necessitated the change in his usual urbane, cynical demeanour. Seeing her at the inn, so obviously in trouble, had alighted protective instincts he hardly knew he possessed. So he was rather kinder to her than he was to the new crop of eligible young ladies pressurised to be agreeable to the rich marquis, to whom he gave only his detached, urbane chatter.

Her terror had kept him kind. That and the knowledge that catching a marquis for a husband was as far from her mind as it could be. At first he attributed this to her extreme youth, but since he had discovered her true age, it was just another of her unique qualities. He sounded like a coxcomb again — of course not every young lady found him tolerable, simply because he was a marquis. He had almost asked Miss Lovatt for another dance, only on the basis of her ill-concealed boredom at that idle chatter he practised to ward off romantic hopes. No, he knew that some young ladies did not find him to their taste. The version of him he displayed at balls and routs, at any rate. But very few. Many more would have liked him because of his position in society even had he been outright rude, he knew.

But Beth *did* like him, he was sure. And yet she evidently did not consider him as a prospective mate. They had developed (in such a short time) a cheerful, teasing tone with each other, and she was not afraid to put him in his place. No, that was not quite right. Concern for others seemed to *compel* her to do so, and she was delightfully guilty afterwards. They all, Emmi, Beth and he, seemed to have meshed. She was not like a guest at all. She was almost like his sister to him.

No, that was a lie. There had been moments between them, such powerful moments when he had felt her tremble beneath his fingers, when her gaze seemed to sear his skin. If he did not kiss her soon, he felt he might explode. But to do so while she was under his protection would be unpardonable. Also, to do so while he was so confused at his feelings for her, would similarly be unpardonable. He would not so wound her tender heart. Since when he had developed such a conscience, he had no idea. How could it be? How *could* he have been entranced by this small creature who, though young, seemed to have such unusual depth in her eyes? Those large, soft, often merry, sometimes angry then quickly guilty, glowing eyes. However it was, he knew. The mystery of her, her covering up whatever scrape she had been in, the reluctance to tell, gave him pause. She *must* confide in him, and before the Horescombes returned. It seemed all at once a test of her regard for him.

But if she would do that, if he knew that it was the same for her as it was for him, he would forget the insanity of falling for a pretty young girl in a matter of probably two days. He knew he desired her, but he knew she was merry and true and a woman of depths that seemed unlikely for her age and gentle rearing. He would like to know the cause of that knowledge, to heal the hurts he saw there, but that was for later. Emmi's pushing them together aside, he realised he'd known on his own. Beth was for him — if only she truly felt for him as he did for her. If she would confide in them, he decided, then he would know.

Now on the road to his club, he decided to turn around and return home, hopeful for a word with her before his sister's return. She was not the normal vision of a siren, but still his heart heard her song.

Chapter 11

Sophy was able to stretch her legs at last, the stage reaching London and depositing its charges at Cheapside, at the Swan with Two Necks. The large cobbled inn yard was bustling with life, ostlers changing horses, and porters moving carts. Sophy, in her plain bonnet, was largely ignored, being pushed rudely aside by a boy helping with the unloading of the luggage. She almost spoke sharply to him, but held her tongue.

It was a large old inn with beamed galleries on the second floor on three sides, where the motley crew of travellers, from farmer to gentleman, were at their leisure to stand on the covered balconies and watch the new stagecoach's arrival. They regarded the excitement, rather as though they were in theatre boxes, watching the performance below. Sophy, looking above, encountered the gaze of watery-eyed gentleman with a pipe in his mouth, leering at her. She wished she might have persuaded Betty to come with her after all, but that young maid had been adamant that she had no need for *Lunnon*.

'Don't you want to see the world, Betty?' had said Sophy, perplexed. 'Don't you want things to happen to you?'

Betty had sniffed. 'Not Lunnon things, miss,' she answered dismissively.

Now, Sophy suddenly felt very small. She had not been in the busiest of London streets before and certainly not in Cheapside. She touched the shoulder of the best dressed man she could find, who wore a rather flashy military uniform, and said, 'Excuse me sir, could you indicate to me the way to —'she realised she did not want to give her direction, '— to Hyde Park?'

The man turned. He sported a natty set of military whiskers, an eye as watery as the leering gentleman's on the gallery, and a disquieting smile that revealed several missing teeth. She saw at once that the uniform was frayed, the gold braid sadly tarnished, and smelt strong spirits emanate from him. She stepped back, but he held her arm. 'Certainly, my pretty, come with me!'

Without making a scene, which might draw the attention of the gentlemen whose carriages were also in the yard, one of whom may discover her disguise, Sophy could hardly get away. She would kick and run if need be, but she was relieved when she heard a voice say, 'Excuse me sir, but I think this is the maid I'm to take to my master's house.'

'What?' The military gentleman looked like he would dispute this, but the man, obviously an upper servant of some kind, was almost a foot taller than he, and looked determined beneath his servility, so he said 'Very well,' and turned away, disgruntled.

'Right you!' said the tall man to Sophy. 'Lost in London, is it? Well, you're in luck, for I have to walk past Hyde Park to get back to my master's. Come with me.' He strode off, rather than trying to manhandle her, and so Sophy ran to catch up with him. As she skipped two steps to match his long stride, the dark servant looked down at her amused, and slowed. 'Where you off to, then? In service?'

'Yes!' said Sophy, 'And I'm going to Grosvenor Square.' She did not wish to say the real street, two blocks from the square.

'You really are in luck then, that's where my lord, the Marquis of Wrexham lives.'

Sophy frowned momentarily. She did not know the marquis, but it would be assured that her guardians did. Grosvenor Square was a little too close to home in case she was recognised. She had noted that she did not draw attention that she usually did in London streets, and was a little lowered to think that it might be the cause of her gown. If the admiration one received was only for one's dress, it was very sad indeed. However, it reduced the chance of being recognised, and for that she was thankful. She would give the tall servant the slip when she saw some place she recognised. They walked for some time, the tall, handsome servant feigning disinterest, but taking a look at her occasionally none the less.

'You're a pretty piece,' he said, eventually. Sophy started. Gentlemen said the same things in a rather more delicate way.

'Lawks!' she said, imitating the chambermaid at Horescombe House.

'Who are you to work for? Don't be afraid, they don't usually bite, and you'll get used to London being so big.'

Sophy held up her nose. 'I've been here before, my lad,' she said, aping Betty's Devon accent, 'I'm a-joining my mistress.'

'You're a bit young to be a lady's maid ain't you?' and Sophy realised that Beth had been so. She supposed it was an achievement for a young girl. 'Well, glad you're in the square,' he winked, 'maybe I'll see you around. What household do you join?'

'Never you mind.'

'Just trying to be friendly.' They walked on for some minutes, through Drury Lane and its theatres, which the young girl seemed to be completely fascinated with. Nevertheless, she moved closer to him, as they passed the painted ladies, the street women with their bawling babes - some reeking of gin, the lolling gutter-snipes, and those men she had heard referred to as 'flash coves', an obscene and gaudy pantomime of real gentlemen.

Her tall companion spoke to take her mind off the poor, crying baby which had indeed made her eyes fill. 'Why are you not with your mistress then?'

'An accident, I had to stay behind when my mistress carried on.'

'What name?'

Sophy said the first name that came into her mind, knowing that it could mean nothing to him. It was not Horescombe, which he might just know as a neighbour to his lord. And then, Sophy had learnt that the nearer one stuck to the truth, the easier it was to remember the lie. 'Miss Ludgate,' she said breezily.

The tall servant stopped. 'You don't mean it? You're Miss Sophy's lost maid?'

Sophy was, for once, totally silenced.

Beth jumped up as she heard the marquis return, setting aside her book. She ran to the hall, where Frost was divesting him of his driving coat.

'Your lordship, I mean Wrexham, I am so glad you have returned. If it is convenient I should like to speak to you.'

He looked down on her, smiling that intimate smile that crinkled the lines around his deep sapphire eyes and softened the harshness of his face. She was almost diverted from her purpose and smiled back a little too widely, quite forgetting her task for a second. He broke the moment, saying, 'It is quite convenient, Miss Fox.'

The brilliance of his smile as he said this, the joy in his face seemed somehow inappropriate,

Beth and the Mistaken Identity

as though he thought she had some good news for him. She noticed Frost frozen for a moment, watching them in a more interested fashion than butlers usually permitted themselves, and was a trifle confused. At any rate, she must finish her errand and she asked enquiringly, tilting her head, 'In the library, my lord?'

He smiled, again with more brilliance than was his wont, and they moved into the room.

'The library will miss you when you are gone, Miss Fox,' he remarked.

'And I it,' said Beth, looking around.

'Have you enjoyed your morning with the Greeks?'

'Well yes, when I was able to concentrate. Only I was diverted by a conversation I had with Dobson before he left. That is what I wanted to discuss with you.' She was looking up at the marquis and saw his eyes dull and his smile fade. 'Are you annoyed with me sir? Do I intrude?'

'No, I merely thought — hoped — that you might be about to discuss another matter with me.' He took a seat on the elegant sofa and crossed his legs, looking more forbidding than she had seen him thus far.

'I — do not understand. What matter?' she said, suddenly nervous.

'Something of rather more importance to me than *domestic matters*,' he said in the same, drawling voice.

His dismissive tone enraged Beth once more,

but she kept her tone clipped by saying, 'There are people behind those *domestic matters* you find so unimportant.' She tried to bite it back, and was surprised to see his eyes alight with the old amusement once more. 'I'm so so—'

'Sorry. I know. You always are after you give me a dressing down. It is most amusing.'

'I can hardly believe the things I say to you. It is just that I have been turning Dobson's words over in my mind—' she blushed, and held her hands together in a penitent pose. 'But it is no excuse. I will discuss whatever you wish.'

'Come, sit,' he said, perhaps a little penitent himself, indicating the place at the other end of the sofa. Beth did so, still a little stiff, but breathing hard at their nearness, the safe distance eaten up by heat. His eyes seemed to drop to her heaving bosom for a fraction of a second and she was ashamed to give away her reaction to him. He grasped one of her little fists and said, 'Oh Beth,' she trembled at his first use of her name, 'pray do not poker up at me again. We are friends are we not?' Her eyes had flown to his at the touch, but though it inflamed her, it comforted as well. His eyes were kind again, and she was able to relax a little. 'I am willing to listen to whatever wonderful plan you have to heal the domestic disasters that I did not even know were fermenting under this roof before you got here, if we can discuss just one thing before we do so.' He smiled and she squeezed his hand a little before he went on, and

Beth and the Mistaken Identity

then removed hers from his.

'Of course.' And she smiled at him then, in almost her old way.

'I wish you could confide in me, Beth. You have said we are friends, and I feel it to be so. Would you not tell a friend your troubles, would you conceal so much from him? I need to know your story, Beth.'

Beth looked at him openly, but sadly. 'All will be known when the Horescombes return on Friday. Can you not be content with that?'

'So on Friday, the Horescombes will explain all to me? I would much rather you did that before. It would let me know that you trust me.' His face was serious, and intense.

Beth looked, and wondered if she could do it. But the look of disgust that she imagined once the truth was told held her silent. She needed the Horescombes to explain what she never could. It was not her place to accuse Miss Sophy, or to blame her for her own stupidity. 'Please believe me, there are reasons, not all mine, that I cannot tell you all just now.' His head dropped, losing contact with her eyes, and a muscle in his jaw moved. 'Perhaps it would be better if I simply left,' she said desolately.

He rose and moved to the fire and stood with his back to her. 'Don't be absurd. All things will be clear when the general returns.'

She regarded his back sadly, feeling like the biggest coward that had ever lived. 'Wrexham —'

He turned and smiled fleetingly. 'No, my dear, I will not press you to say more. It is unkind of me. Now! Tell me what domestic disaster you wish to avert.'

She matched his pretence that nothing had changed, told him, in carefully chosen words, the gist of her conversation with Dobson.

'So you think that I need appoint an under-housekeeper? Why does Mrs Fitch not simply retire? Good God, she has been in my employ long enough to know that no awful fate awaits my old retainers. She will have a snug cottage on one of my estates and a pension. She has nought to fear.'

'You do not understand. Mrs Fitch is terrified of ceasing to be useful when the truth is, she is still of great value in your home. There is much more to a housekeeper's responsibilities, you know, such as the household accounts and the running of staff, than walking up the stairs to see that maids have performed their duties. And it seems to me that Meg, long trained by Mrs Fitch, would be ably qualified to do that task.'

'So you have already chosen my under-housekeeper?' He laughed indulgently, even more like himself.

'I do not even know her, sir. I am going by the advice of Dobson, who does,' said Beth contritely, but with a little of her teasing tone.

'What I do not understand, is that if this Meg is able to check the other maids, why on earth is she not doing so now?'

'There is a little jealousy on the part of Mrs Fitch. At this time of weakness she fears being usurped. And if one does not have the authority, you know, it is tantamount to starting a battle to instruct other servants.'

He sighed. 'I do not wish to know all this domestic detail. I need a wife to deal with these matters.'

Beth blushed, and was shaken once more. But it was necessary to continue her task. His eyes seemed to linger on her blush in a questioning way that she feared. 'Just one more thing. When you discuss the matter with Mrs Fitch—'

He smiled a lazy and frightening smile, returning to the sofa, to her uneasiness. '— and you think I will obey you as usual?' he teased.

She could not help responding to his teasing as she always did, saying in the tone she would use to admonish her brother's starts, 'Of course you will. It is for your own benefit, after all. You must assure her that you cannot dispense with her services, so well has she run your house. But you have become aware of her illness, and understand that for physical tasks *only*, she requires some support, so you have determined to appoint Meg to the position of under-housekeeper. *Strictly* under her supervision.' Beth looked at him, still lazily smiling. 'Here is the most delicate part of the interview —' he adopted a riveted expression, which she sent a quelling look to, 'You must be a trifle devious I think. Before Mrs Fitch can repudiate the need for help, you will inform her that if she doesn't accept the support, you will reluctantly have to send her to the country, because you could not have on your conscience the collapse of her health in your service.'

'Inspired! I shall tell Dobson to convey those very words to Mrs Fitch as soon as he returns.'

'Oh, no — it must be *you*, my lord.'

His shoulders fell, 'Why on earth—'

'I assure you, anyone else but you would not carry the case. She would fear that Dobson was against her, and had informed on her. Or Cook or another would bear the blame.'

'Thus causing future ructions,' he said, defeated. 'Very well, Miss Fox. It shall be I.'

Her smiled glowed again, and for a moment he bent toward her. He hovered close and Beth felt she might never breathe again, but after a few seconds, he lifted a curl that had drifted close to her eye. He held it for a second seeming entranced by it, and Beth finally let out her breath. 'Beth, please —' he began. Her lips parted and trembled, she was locked in those deep sapphire eyes, a colour she had never seen before in a person. She could look nowhere else. She did not know what he begged of her, but the answer in her heart was yes. His eyes both questioned and enticed, but there was a place in them where she could lose herself forever — had already. They were frozen in the moment, Wrexham still holding her curl, and it was thus that the princess found them.

Emmeline, pushing the ajar library door fully open, was saying, 'Beth, you must come and see —' She paused, taking in the quick parting of her brother, who had seemed to be holding a curl of Beth's hair, and an embarrassed Beth.

'Tobias!' she said in the tone of a shocked duenna. 'What are you about, being alone with Beth?'

'The door was—' protested her brother.

'Ajar. I know. But that does not excuse this proximity to Beth.'

Beth was blushing furiously now, saying, 'Oh but there was nothing—'

The princess raised her eyebrows, standing over them, now at the very opposite ends of the small sofa, '*Nothing*, you say? And how is it neither of you heard my arrival? Or my chatting to Frost as I took off my bonnet and arranged for the disposal of my parcels? The door is *ajar,* as you have so recently reminded me, Tobias, and yet I find you as close as any married couple.'

Wrexham shot his sister a look of warning for her physical being, but she continued. 'I was never more shocked!' Beth could hardly look at Wrexham, but he said warningly to his sister, 'Emmi, if you don't stop this at once –'

Suddenly his sister whirled, and sat between them on the sofa, grasping the hand of each. 'Oh my dears, I am so very happy. I knew this would happen from the very first!'

'Emmi!' said the marquis urgently, while Beth uttered, 'I assure you it is not what you think—'

But there had been a new arrival in the hallway, not from the front door but from the servants' quarters, which they did hear this time. Dobson was saying in a low voice outside the door, 'Wait there, you!' Then he entered in a stately fashion. 'Your lordship,' he said now. 'I believe I have some good news.'

The marquis, who had feared a fresh domestic disaster, and had been grateful for the interruption nevertheless, stood and moved forward. 'Indeed, Dobson? I think I stand in need of good news just now.'

'I believe I have found Miss Lu— Miss Fox's lost maid.'

Beth's mind froze for a moment, standing too. How on earth could—? But it was absurd, a mistake. Her voice shook as she said, 'Ind-deed?'

'Yes miss!' He allowed himself a slight smile as he looked at Beth, 'Shall I bring her in?'

And Beth, so sure there was some dreadful mistake, could never have expected Sophy Ludgate, wearing some awful stuff gown, bobbing her a curtsy in the doorway. Beth collapsed in the nearest chair.

The marquis saw a pretty young blond in an exceptionally dull dress, bobbing Beth a curtsy, with a kind of impish look on her face that was quite arresting, if hardly appropriate for her position.

'Oh, Miss Sophy,' she was saying to Beth, 'I am ever so pleased to have found you again.'

Beth's mouth moved but no sound came out, and Wrexham was intrigued.

'Hah! I told you so Wrexham!' said his sister. But then she frowned slightly. 'Did you not then, break your leg?'

The girl blinked, then said with aplomb, 'Oh, no, my lady. It turned out to be a bad sprain only.'

'Very fortunate,' drawled the marquis. 'As was your discovery of your mistress's location.'

'I was fortunate to meet your butler, my lord, who offered to show me to Hyde Park, me not knowing that part of Lunnon, sir.'

There was something pert about this maid. Although the tone in the thick country accent was servile, something in her dancing eyes, which she cast down occasionally, made him suspicious. Beth's frozen aspect did not detract from this. She seemed fixated on her maid as though to a vision, and could not manage to speak.

'Hyde Park?'

'Well, I fancied Miss Sophy might have gone home to Horescombe House, my lord, and I would know my way from the park.' She cast those laughing eyes down again, 'and I didn't want to give no strange Lunnon men my direction.'

Dobson became even stiffer at this, looking down his nose at the maid.

'I hope you have Miss F - Miss Ludgate's baggage.'

The maid opened those pert eyes wide, trying

for innocence that Wrexham did not believe.

'Oh, no my lord, there were too many trunks. So many fine dresses does Miss Sophy take on her journeys. It is to be sent on once I was certain of Miss Sophy's direction.'

Again, an inarticulate noise came from Beth, or Sophy, as he must accustom himself to think of her. She was blushing and shaking profusely.

His sister was set on wrinkling out the details. 'I thought you believed her to be at Horescombe House?'

'Well, as to that milady, it wasn't quite decided,' she appeared to take a fearful look at her mistress and added in a conciliating tone, 'Miss Sophy having so many friends in Lunnon.'

The marquis looked at Beth, concerned.

'Very well. You may go,' said the marquis with a nod to Dobson, who had to touch the girl's shoulder to make her obey. She was looking at Beth with a blank look that he thought hid merriment. Obviously, only part of the mystery of Beth — Sophy — had been revealed, but he would not insult her by interrogating her maid in her presence.

He looked at Beth now.

She found her voice at last. 'Wait!' she said, 'Send her to my room, if you please, I wish to speak with her.'

The maid, almost out the door, had the temerity to raise her brows at this, and a hint of a grin passed her face, before she quelled it. She bobbed a curtsy once more. 'Yes, miss.' She said with that pert manner.

'What a dreadful dress she was wearing Sophy,' said the princess.

Beth appeared to jump and uttered 'Please call me Beth...'

His sister was continuing, apparently missing much of what he had seen, '—do you not give her your old gowns? Or is she just an abigail, rather than your lady's maid? She has a very countrified appearance. But rather pretty, I thought.'

Beth seemed for a second to exhibit relief, but it was not long before the tightness returned. Why could she not tell him now, Wrexham thought. She must know what he felt. He watched her keeping her secrets, holding them in her tightly woven fingers, still not trusting him. It made him frustrated and angry. But the terror in her face, which she sought to mask with a closed expression, inclined him to her again, making him want to protect her from whatever haunted her.

'She is not so long in my employ,' she said answering the mild enquiry of his sister. 'Now, if you do not mind, I would like to speak to my maid.'

'I shall order tea at the half hour Sophy — Beth, if you prefer. Don't be late. And afterwards I shall show you the glorious silks I bought today.'

'Yes. Very well.'

The marquis noted her eagerness to be off, such that her body was inclined forward, her hands poised to pick up her skirts, though her feet were rooted to the ground.

'With your permission, my lord,' she said, with the briefest, most painful look in his eyes.

He inclined his head. She curtsied, then picked up her skirts and almost ran from the room.

'Well, that is the mystery settled,' Emmi was saying as he regarded the door she had left through. Then she added carelessly. 'But why must I still call her Beth? I own it will be difficult to call her Sophy after all this time,' she prattled, but the marquis was deep in thought. His Beth was in trouble. How could he help if he did not know what it was? 'Perhaps,' continued Emmi, 'her real name is Sophia Elizabeth.' She looked at him brightly and he suddenly paid attention.

'You are foolish beyond measure, Emmi, can you not see that Beth is in some real trouble?'

Chapter 12

Beth almost raced up the stairs to see Miss Sophy. She'd had only one more day to go before she could feel *clean* again, free of the lies that she had let them believe. And now the devil had arrived and whatever else she knew, she knew no good could come of it. She was stopped from genuinely sprinting, as she had had to in fulfilling Miss Badger's will on regular occasions, by the presence of footmen in the hall. She reached her room and threw open the door to find Miss Sophy lying negligently on the *chaise longue*, scratching her shoulder.

'This dress is very itchy,' she uttered in an off-hand way, 'I can't think how Betty stands it.'

Beth had come to a halt and by rote had taken up her customary posture in Miss Sophy's presence, very straight and with her hands clasped in front of her.

'Betty—?' asked Beth, her thoughts all at sea.

Miss Sophy smiled and sat up, 'The maid that I exchanged this with for that lovely pink muslin. You know the one, Beth.' She leaned forward and patted the sofa. 'Come and let me tell you of my adventures,' she added enthusiastically, 'I have been on the stage, you know. Not very comfortable, but vastly amusing!'

Beth sat, not knowing how to deal with any of this. She was nervous, and many other emotions were choking her. A bare half hour ago, she had been only an inch away from Wrexham's face, falling into his eyes, and now she was the maid again, fearful of what her mistress might say or do next. She had raced upstairs to confront her, to ask her what new madness this was, but halfway to the room, she remembered who she was once more.

'Beth, 'said Miss Sophy, 'Why do you look so gloomy? Do you fear I will tattle on you? We are friends, are we not? Do tell me how you started masquerading as me. How clever of you. You know, when I was getting a peal rung over me for not worrying about you, I *told* them you would be fine. And you are!' She leaned over and gave Beth a quick hug. 'Not that I could have guessed you would be living in such splendour. A marquis! Tell me how you managed it.'

Beth resented Miss Sophy's sanguine account of her prospects, at the same time as being caught up in her affection. 'I did not *manage* it Miss, it just — just happened.' Sophy's eyes widened, a rapt listener. 'I suppose it is because you *do* dress me better than, er, Betty.'

'What were you wearing?' said Sophy, enthralled.

'The blue pelisse miss, and this dress,' said Beth, 'But the point is, that as I was waiting to apply to the landlord for a position, a gentleman — the marquis, mistook me for a lady, or at least a schoolgirl of gentle birth. He procured me a room, which I, in my pride, had demanded of the landlord. It was in the evening, and though I could hardly afford it, I knew, by regarding the inn, that it was not the correct position for me.'

'Yes, yes, but how come you to be living *here, and* under my name?'

'I have never claimed to be you miss, I swear. Indeed, I denied it.'

'To whom?'

'The princess, miss.'

Sophy laughed. 'Now you are jesting, Beth. There cannot be a *princess* in this fairy-tale.'

'Indeed there is, Miss Sophy. The marquis's sister is a widowed princess, but lately returned to town from Europe. She had seen us that dreadful — that night at Vauxhall Gardens, miss. She admired the dress I was wearing from afar, and asked someone who the lady in pink was.'

'And they said Sophy Ludgate, because I was wearing the pink domino!' Miss Sophy said brilliantly then added thoughtfully, 'Perhaps we shouldn't have taken off our masks...'

Beth's temper rose, but she merely said, 'No miss.'

'So the princess thought I was you, and the marquis offered to drive me to London, and since it was my best hope of finding a situation, I agreed.'

'Well, how splendid. But why are you in the marquis's house still?'

'It was difficult to get away from him, miss,' said Beth, less sure of her ground. 'I had given my name as Elizabeth Fox, ma'am, but the princess would not shake the notion that I was you. Because of your reputation, miss.' Beth looked to see how Miss Sophy took this, but she was nothing but interested. 'She feared I had run away from my guardians. And the marquis refused to let me go until he could hand me to my family.'

'That is the chivalrous thing to do, I suppose. I do not expect that they could release you in all conscience. Those dreadful proprieties again,' she sighed. 'I expect you would have a position by now if you were not so caught.'

'Girls without a character find it very hard to find a position, miss,' said Beth repressively.

Miss Sophy looked surprised at Beth's hint of disdain. 'Oh, but you are so very clever, Beth. You sew so well and do hair delightfully. I knew you would be alright.' Beth swallowed. Miss Sophy would never understand. 'And what happened next?'

I fell in love, thought Beth wonderingly, but with someone so far above me that it is ridiculous. But she said instead, 'They sent a message to Horescombe House miss, as they believed me to be you.' Beth looked earnestly at her mistress, 'I never told them so, Miss Sophy. I denied it vehemently.'

'Vehemently! Your vocabulary is improving, Beth, and your accent is truly marvellous. See how my tutelage saw you through this adventure?'

'Yes, miss.'

'I can guess what is next. The Horescombes had left town to punish me with the most dreadful house party you can imagine, all the way in Devon. And so finding this out, the marquis resolved to keep you until the general returned.'

'Yes, miss. I knew I should have escaped, but by this time I could not repay their care of me by worrying them.'

'Worry — why, whatever can you mean?'

Beth had heard enough from her erstwhile mistress to know that worry for her maid had not featured in her thoughts, and made haste to defend her friends, 'The marquis and Her Serene Highness are unusually kind, my lady. I feared to wound them.'

Miss Sophy gave her that pert regard. 'I expect that you mean more tender-hearted than *I*. I have said sorry for dragging you into a scrape, Beth. And what is more,' she added piously, 'I had determined, when I inherited, or became married, that I would look for you and re-engage you!'

Beth wondered what would have happened, what still might happen, in the years before that occurred. She shuddered to think of herself becoming a tavern wench, or worse. The alternative, unless she could earn her living by stitching, was to starve to death. But she merely said, 'Thank you miss.' She needed to change the subject before she showed her anger. 'But how did you find me miss?'

'Oh, I had run away from the dreadful house party, just to teach the general and Lady Ernestine a lesson, you know, and determined to go home until they returned.'

Beth's face was grave.

'Oh, do not be a fusspot, Beth. I dressed in this awful gown so that I would not be accosted. It is the first time I have ever been unchaperoned, do you realise? It was quite a heady experience. And there were such droll characters on the stage ... but I will tell you all later. The point is, when I met your butler, he asked whose maid I was, and since I did not know what other servants he might know, I thought the safest name to say was my own. When he told me Sophy Ludgate was residing with his master, I did not know what to think. But of course I had to come.' She smiled joyfully, then paused. 'But if you are Miss Fox here, how came he to believe you were I?'

Beth did not take long to think of this. 'I expect he was in the room when the master and his sister were discussing it. No one ever notices servants.'

'There is a change in you, Beth. And it not just in the new hairstyle. I am not surprised that you have passed for a lady. How very cross the marquis will be when he finds out.'

Beth looked tortured and Miss Sophy leaned forward and took her hand. 'Don't be worried Beth, I have people cross with me all the time. It doesn't last forever.'

'I thought — I hardly know, but I thought that Lady Ernestine, on her return tomorrow might be able to explain my predicament —' she put her head down and raised it again. 'No, I know it was wrong. I should have told them the truth as soon as I reached London.'

'You should, of course,' said Miss Sophy piously, 'but I expect you were enjoying the adventure too much.' There was nothing to say to this. 'I think it an adventure to be a lady's maid. We shall have such fun, Beth. I shall be you, and you me, for a few days at least. And the general shall pay for that dull party and know that he must not try me. And I shall be chaperoned by *you* all the time, so he cannot say I have ruined my reputation. But we had best not go out much. I may be recognised.'

Beth, who had jumped up at the mention of more deception, was striding the floor. 'We cannot do this! Your family will be desperately worried. I have been a cowardly fool, but this I will not tolerate.'

Miss Sophy pulled herself up. 'You forget yourself, Beth. You will do as I demand.'

Beth froze. 'No, I shall tell the marquis this minute. You are not my mistress any longer.' She turned swiftly and headed for the door, but the swift figure of Miss Sophy caught her, and held her arm.

'Beth, Beth, you are overwrought. Stop a minute and think. The Horescombes will return this evening, but very late. What harm is there in waiting at least until tomorrow, as you had planned?' Her manner changed a little. 'I quite forgive you for speaking to me in that tone, for your nerves have been stretched since you left Foster Hall, and I am aware that some of that is my fault. Let me be your maid for tonight, Beth. It will be so droll.'

There was no point in arguing with her, Beth knew. 'I must go now, E— the princess is serving tea.'

Miss Sophy looked perplexed for a moment, but then said in her energetic way, 'Oh, very good. Continue the charade as we planned. Tea with a princess, Beth! You must be transported with joy.' Beth headed for the door, saying nothing. 'Oh,' said Miss Sophy, lying back on the chaise longue, 'have tea and bread and butter sent up, will you? I haven't had anything since breakfast.'

Beth turned and said, in as even a voice as she could manage, 'It would be very odd to have tea sent to my maid. I suggest you beg the indulgence of Mrs Bates in the kitchen. I shall tell Dobson I wish you to be fed.'

'To the manor born, Beth. It's a bother going to the kitchen, but I suppose it may be interesting. Tell Dobson — how amusing!' She laughed good-naturedly, and Beth breathed heavily.

'Yes miss.' She swept a curtsy, but as she rose she realised it had not been deep enough for a servant

Beth and the Mistaken Identity

to a lady. But as she left the bedroom, she found she did not care.

Emmi called to her as she passed the open door of the green salon, 'Beth, tea is on its way. You are practically late.'

'I shall be there directly, Your Highness, I have a note to write.'

'Don't be long delayed or it will be cold.'

Beth smiled briefly, 'I will be but a moment.'

She headed to the library, where she knew she might find writing materials on his lordship's desk. She was surprised to see him there and stopped at the entrance.

They looked at each other directly, across the length of the room, and Beth felt unable to move. They were locked thus for perhaps a minute, until the marquis said, not dropping his eyes, 'Have you come to tell me your secrets now, my Beth?'

How could he call her that? Her heart swelled, she thought now that to be torn from him would be to leave her bleeding for all her life. But at what she saw in his face she now feared worse — that she would be the means of wounding him, too. The tears rolled down her face as she looked at him.

'I cannot, my lord, I am too much a coward, and I have deceived you too much.'

He dropped his head then, but Beth thought she saw a gleaming drop of water hit some paper before him. 'Why then?' he said harshly.

'I wished to write a note and end one lie at least.'

'The Horescombes? Very well,' he said, passing her on his way to the door. She had jumped aside as though he might burn her, she gave a sob and then stiffened her spine. She emerged from the library in but a minute, and handed Dobson an unsealed sheet. 'Have this note delivered to Horescombe House, if you please, Dobson. Immediately.'

He bowed and looked into her face, but she was as expressionless as she could be.

'My maid may be in the kitchen. Could you ask Cook to see she is fed?'

'Certainly miss.' She smiled at him briefly, to soften the formality of her speech.

She moved to the green salon where Emmi was pouring tea, and beginning to chastise her lateness, stopping when she saw her face. 'But Beth, whatever troubles you? You are pale as death.'

'I am quite alright.'

She joined Emmi on the couch, waiting while she poured the tea. 'Well, now that we know who you truly are, Beth, will you not consent to tell me the rest?'

Beth stopped her arm raising the cup and saucer and brought her hand down to rest with hers. 'Oh, Emmi, it is not long before you find out about the dreadful — liberties — I have taken by allowing you to befriend me.'

'Liberties?' declared Emmi, 'What on earth are you talking about Beth? You must tell me all, I *command* it.'

'Please do not. Tomorrow—'

'We will know all! I know, I know. You keep telling me so.' She pouted in an exaggerated way, 'But princesses are not accustomed to waiting for what they desire.'

Beth smiled. 'But you are so far above other princesses.'

'You know so many, Madame?' Emmi smiled back.

'No, but I know that you are far above any human being of my acquaintance, and that suffices.'

Emmi looked touched. 'What has brought on your strange mood, Beth? Don't you know that Wrexham and I will stand your friend whatever you say?' She stopped, looking worried. 'Unless — Beth, tell me you are not married. I think that might break him.'

'He has no such feelings for me,' said Beth with a faux lightness, trying to convince herself as well as her friend. 'But no, I am not married.' She looked at Emmi who was smiling once more. 'I tell you it makes no odds. *Please* do not make me tell you all tonight. I hope for one more dinner together, before it ends.' Despite herself, she sobbed.

'Beth, Beth there is no need for this...'

Beth's head came up. 'I must tell you this at least. 'I have practised a cruel deception, I have been very wicked indeed. But never think that I have deceived you in my enjoyment of your friendship, in my appreciation of your kindness. I do not think I will get a chance to say this tomorrow. I fear you will be too angry to hear me.'

'Beth Fox! Or Ludgate ... have some tea and let us talk no more nonsense. You are worried about your reputation or some such, but my brother and I have considerable influence. I will probe you no more, and after tea I will show you my silks, and we will cheer you up. All will be well, I assure you.'

Beth looked at her sadly. 'All is well for just now,' she agreed, drinking her tea.

The rest of the day went in a whirl, Beth's head pounding in her sorrow. She knew this day would come, but she thought that there was this one day left, before the dreadful disappointment and the shock and disgust of her friends. She wanted to save some joy from today, though she knew she did not deserve it. She would serve her penance later. It was salved by the joy that Emmi showed when sharing her newest acquisition. She oooh and aaaahed at the lengths of silks, the sketches of the gowns they would soon become. 'You sketched these?' said Beth wonderingly.

'Well yes, I had an idea of some gowns that I loved in Paris, and Madame Godot can give them some more interest.'

'You are so talented Emmi! What a designer you would have made!'

Emmi blushed and laughed. 'Make my living as a seamstress? Oh, Beth you are so amusing.'

Beth blushed. 'Silly. But it is just such a talent

Emmi, going to waste.'

'It is not wasted, for I design for myself as I will for you my dear. I can just see you in a pale green crape, tucked at the bodice you know, and—'

'Madame must on no account wear this turquoise,' interrupted Cécile, lifting up a length of silk.

The princess raised an eyebrow. 'That will be all, Cécile.'

The maid gave her a pert look and bustled out in a rustle of silk, muttering to herself in French.

'She is a dear, my Cécile, but she sometimes seeks to rule my choices. Isn't it lovely?' she asked, picking up the satin.

'Beautiful, but not for you, Emmi.'

The princess opened her mouth and shut it again. 'You are in a conspiracy against me.' She went to the gilt mirror and held the fabric in front of her. 'Oh blast, to use Wrexham's phrase, I suppose you are both right. Now Cécile will be intolerably smug.' She looked at Beth, 'I shall have it made up for you, and sent to Horescombe House. I shall design something simple and maidenly — which I admit will test my powers — and you will look divine in it. She was holding it against Beth now, and Beth hugged her impulsively.

'Oh Emmi, how kind you are. And what a beast I am.' She rose suddenly as the princess called her name. 'I must go. I will see you at dinner.'

'Back to your fusty old book, I suppose,' said Emmi, shaken, but determinedly smiling.

Beth only smiled and left.

She could not, of course, go to the library, lest she meet Wrexham. At dinner, with Emmi, she looked forward to seeing him, hopeful that with her help they could fall into their usual relations. It was much to hope for, but she treasured it. So, she went to her room, where she found Sophy unexpectedly sewing.

'Beth! Thank goodness. Order some refreshment will you, I'm quite parched, and that tartar of a housekeeper was set on putting me to work if I remained in the kitchen. I was quite wonderfully deceptive... I called myself Sally Brown and tried to make friends with them all. I must say, some of the footmen are rougher in their speech than they are above stairs. But the cook was not kind at all, either. After only some tea, toast and a very old slice of cheese that I was so hungry I ate, she told me that was sufficient. When I told her I was still hungry, she boxed my ears.' She looked at Beth wide-eyed. 'Is this the sort of treatment you receive at Foster Hall?'

Food was not on constant call for the servants, and they received what was left. No cook would let her staff eat at will. And talking back to this high individual was severely punished. Beth knew not to do so, but she said with a quiet satisfaction to Miss Sophy, 'Yes.'

'How dreadful. Well, anyway, I preserved my rôle and apologised, though I longed to strike her. And then I said I must tend to Miss Beth's things and left. Do you ring, Beth. Order some bread and some ham perhaps, and cheese — definitely cheese.' She laughed. 'They will not serve Miss Sophia Ludgate such stuff as they gave me. And then the old hag of a housekeeper gave me linen to mend and I was so bored when you were gone that I began. But I do not think I set my stitches well.' Beth looked and could not but agree. It was quite dreadful. 'Never mind, Beth, you may take the stitches out and finish it, then she will be content with me.' She thrust the work at Beth, who automatically sat down to do as she was bid.

'Ring first, Beth! I do not know what horrors I shall be served at the servants' table, so I needs must have something to sustain me. I cannot imagine why servants are not better fed.'

You cannot imagine a great deal of things, thought Beth, ringing the bell. She looked at her young mistress, she was bright and lively, and sometimes kind, but utterly self-absorbed. 'Let them eat cake,' Queen Marie Antoinette had reportedly said, when told that the revolt stemmed from lack of bread for the populace. Not cruel, as some had believed. Just the same as Miss Sophy, utterly unaware of other people's struggles, excepting in the vaguest way possible. Tomorrow, she, Beth, would be cast off. She still had the remains of the sovereign that Miss Sophy had given her, and the hope of part of her wages at the end of the quarter. With her coins, she could perhaps afford some mean room, so that she had an address to have her box and her wages sent on. When the box arrived, perhaps she could sell some of the gowns that Miss Sophy had been so kind as to give to her, for shillings instead of the pounds they cost. She could walk the streets looking for a position, in fear of violent attack from men, and if she could not get one, perhaps she could take in sewing for fourteen hours a day, as her mother's friend did, only able to work when she could afford the tallow candles. She would become shabby without the means to wash so often, and hungry. Perhaps she might break down and allow a man to take advantage of her. If she were ever to do so, it might be better to make this decision now, while she still looked respectable, so that that man might just be a gentleman, able to keep her in comfort. That way, the fall would be slower, she knew. But the fall would come. All she wanted was to work, and keep her respectability. And Miss Sophy's whim for Vauxhall Gardens had taken that from her. She knew she had agreed, but ... Don't excuse yourself, Beth, she thought. It is your fault too. But Miss Sophy now chattering about the shock she was continuing to give to Lady Ernestine, who *deserved* it — and Beth was glad at least, that her note would spare them more pain this evening. The earl, Lady Ernestine and the two dear Misses Fosdyke, would be beside themselves on the journey, worried about what could occur to Miss Sophy on her own, imagining disasters that Sophy did not conceive of. The girl's petty revenge was but a game to her, and she did not realise fully what pain she caused.

Dinner in the kitchen would be good, Beth knew. The old cheese had merely been to put the new girl in her place. As Aggie entered, looking astonished at Sophy, sitting while her mistress stood, Beth shoved her sewing back in her old mistress's hand. 'That is quite alright, Sally, continue.' She turned to Aggie with a smile. 'I'm afraid I made little of breakfast today, and find myself still hungry. Please find something from the kitchen for me. Some bread, some ham perhaps, and of course some cheese.' Aggie looked a little surprised, but bobbed a curtsy, 'Oh and some lemonade, if cook has some by.'

'To be sure she does, miss.'

'Good then.' Aggie turned to leave and Beth opened her mouth and did a saintly thing. 'Oh and have Dobson send up a truckle bed, I wish my maid to sleep in my chamber this evening.' It might have given her the lowest sort of pleasure to let Miss Sophy experience the servants' garret. Rough cold sheets, hard beds, and perhaps a single blanket, especially if the housekeeper was displeased with the pert new maid. But she could not do it.

'Oh Beth, that was inspired!' said Miss Sophy. 'I am very sleepy, and that bed is the finest I have ever seen. Much more elegant than my bed in Horescombe House, or even Foster Hall.' She looked at Beth, smiling. I suppose your comfort will suffer a little, but you do not mind, do you?'

'Not at all,' said Beth truthfully, 'But we have to exchange before Aggie comes in in the morning to light the fire.'

'An honoured guest! And you have adopted my manner perfectly! How amusing. Now you must tell me all about the marquis and the princess. What are their characters? I declare they are a handsome pair. His face is a trifle harsh perhaps, but so masculine, and his dress is elegant. And she! What style she has. I could actually die to wear that dress she was wearing. Has it been awkward? Do they look at you down their noses and pucker up? They must have felt burdened by an unwanted guest, but perhaps were too polite to show it.'

Beth's eyes filled.

'Oh, Beth, don't be so tender. You have been very naughty and I suppose they will be disgusted when once they hear, but we could just run away tomorrow and they might never even know!'

Beth regarded her with amazement. 'And have them worry about me, or believe me so lost in all feeling as to fail to thank them for their kindness?'

'You may leave a note. And then you will not see their rage!'

Beth was almost tempted by this idea. This was Miss Sophy's devilish genius. She persuaded one to ignore their own conscience, for she had none herself. Beth had her honest plan and she would stick to it. But she let Miss Sophy's remarks go, perhaps appearing to agree. It was best Miss Sophy did not guess.

Beth and the Mistaken Identity

So when the food arrived, she let her prattle on, and answered her questions about the household without truly confiding in her. It was time then to dress for dinner, and Beth changed, wrestling with the tiny buttons at her back. Miss Sophy, eventually noticing, sprang up to help. 'Oh, Beth, fancy *me* dressing *you*.' Beth smiled at this. Her mistress was really not unkind, just heedless. 'Your hair needs attending to, I think.'

'I'll see to it,' said Beth, rather regretting the deft hand of Aggie.

'I have no idea what to do until the servants' dinner, so late.'

'Whatever you do,' said Beth in a commanding tone, 'Do not touch that sewing.'

'I shall not,' Miss Sophy laughed, 'Mistress.'

'There is a book on the nightstand,' she offered before she left.

'Oh, I think I will just lie down, it has been such an exciting day.'

'Do not be late for the servants' table,' Beth warned, 'or Mrs Fitch will punish you and cook may not feed you at all.'

'Very well,' said Miss Sophy, already settled on the coverlet, 'miss.' She shut her eyes.

As Beth went downstairs, she saw Dobson at the foot, and moved to talk to him.

'I think you know I am to leave tomorrow, Dobson. I wish to thank you for all you have done for me, and to ask one other service.'

'Anything in my power, Miss Ludgate.'

Beth shivered a little at the name, but continued.

'Tomorrow, the family and I will go to Horescombe House in the carriage after breakfast. My maid will accompany us.'

Dobson bowed. 'You must keep the destination from the staff, in case my maid hears of it. She will not wish to go.' Beth knew Miss Sophy well enough to understand she would hatch a plan to stay if she could.

The butler's mobile brows lifted. It was not a maid's place to have preferences.

She touched his sleeve. 'George,' she said in a more intimate voice, 'you are intelligent enough to know all is not as it seems. I cannot tell you everything, but I must ask this service. Have two footmen near the carriage for the moment that my maid hears the destination. She must go, but she's a bolter!'

She moved away then, and felt Dobson's questioning eyes on her back.

The marquis and his sister were seated, and he stood as she joined him, her seat set by a footman, whom she acknowledged by a smile. She looked at Emmi, smiling but worried, she could see, and then at him. He was avoiding her eye and her heart contracted. Please give me this! she thought. It amazed her that she could hurt him so, that she could move him at all. Her gaze took in his dear, strong face, and she wished she could help him. He would be in more pain tomorrow, but the disclosure of her dire secret would ensure his quicker recovery. He could not mourn for a maid.

Chapter 13

When she came into the room, the marquis followed Beth with his eyes, but only while she was turned away. The footman seated her on his left, and he saw the brief smile she gave the man in gratitude. Everything fine about her. She gave dignity to that simple gown he had seen so often, her hair was casually arranged, her sweet face and lovely eyes his sheer delight. She was natural and unaffected when she smiled at Emmi, as she had been for most of the time after the first day of her visit. When she stopped being stiff and afraid, she had blossomed into a teasing beauty, the width of her glowing smile had caught at his heart. The more he admired her, the more she angered him. Why could she not show her trust in him by confiding?

Emmi had reproached him this afternoon, reminding him that as it was Beth's last night, she was to be indulged and he must stop looking like a brooding poet and oppressing everyone. Her last night. Why did both he and Emmi talk of this as though it were their last ever meeting, as though they were mourning her already? Horescombe House was only some six squares away. Visits, for Emmi at least, were entirely possible. But somehow, it did not feel this way, it felt that she was to be torn from their little group forever. Emmi had any number of friends, but none like Beth. With them, she was as confiding of her personal life as he was, which was to say, not at all. Emmi, trying now to smile to cover the grief in her eyes, made his heart contract in pity. She turned to him, and he gave his attention to the first course.

Beth's voice broke through Emmi's chatter. 'You know how thankful to both of you I am for all you have—'

'Now Beth, you know I have had enough of your thanks and you know it has been a pleasure.' The princess dashed a tear away. 'Now you said you wanted a normal dinner for tonight, and that is what we shall have. No talk of tomorrow. And you, Wrexham,' she said to her stiff brother, 'shall comport yourself.'

Wrexham sighed, playing with the stem of his glass, 'Very well,' he drawled. He looked at Beth and she smiled nervously, an almost pleading look in her eye. 'I *will*!' he conceded, 'I promise!' She gave a twisted smile in return and he was satisfied. Oh, my Beth. Trust me.

There was then a silence of about three minutes, which was so pregnant that they all broke it with a laugh. 'Oh dear,' said the princess, 'I'm afraid I cannot think what a normal dinner consists of!'

Beth laughed shakily and said, 'Well, you talk of your day's purchases, and the latest *on dits* from the friends you met in town,' instructed Beth.

'And I?' asked he.

She looked at him shyly, 'Well, you laugh at Emmi and tease her for being a gossip and express no interest in her purchases, and then she chides you as a mere man. But then *you* talk gossip too,' he raised his brows, 'about the club, or horses, or gambling losses.' His brows were still up. 'Just because it is not from the mouth of a female, it still remains gossip.' She was teasing him a little and she saw the answering warmth in his eyes.

'I sound a very boring kind of fellow,' he remarked.

'Oh no, you also talk of your estate, and your tenants, and I find that very interesting.'

'You are a very strange creature, Beth, to be interested in that. And also the servants and the old books,' Emmi remarked.

He saw Beth look around her at the servants when they were mentioned. No doubt in case they reacted. But they all stood upright in their positions, ready to whisk away their plates and serve the next course. He supposed it *was* rather bad form to talk of them in their presence, but he could not say he had given it any thought before.

Emmi was running on, 'I sound rather empty-headed in your description, I must say.'

'We-ell...,' teased Beth. Then she laughed at

Beth and the Mistaken Identity

Emmi's fallen face. 'You are very kind about your friends and charitable when you hear of a scandal. So I do not think you empty-headed at all.'

'Beth,' smiled Emmi warmly, 'you are a dear. Well, as it seems my duty, I must tell you what happened when I ran into vile old Viscountess Swanson at the silk drapers.'

They were back on their usual road, and Emmi made them laugh while Beth and he teased her. On more than one occasion, their eyes met, laughing. It was so long ago that he had thought her merely pretty. She was his one beauty, and this could not stop tonight, it must not. This was where she belonged, as his marchioness. But was that even what she wanted? Emmi had told him the deception did not include a husband, but who was to say another liaison did not exist — some other man. He ground his teeth.

But he, too, was enjoying tonight too much. They had given her last dinner, and when they parted, she clasped both their hands, standing in a circle with them. 'Thank you,' she said simply, and ran up the stairs.

He stood looking after her, frozen for a moment. He felt Emmi's hand on his arm, her body near him comfortingly. 'Do not, Toby. We will know all tomorrow. She had her reasons for not telling us, but she is young, we must not forget that. She fears consequences that cannot be repaired. But we know that is not so.'

He put his hand on hers, his eyes still fixated on

the stairs, though Beth was no more to be seen. He thought of one problem that could not be repaired: her loving another. But he patted Emmi's hand and they moved towards the stairs, to make their way to bed.

The next morning, Beth packed her few belongings and those even more meagre of her erstwhile mistress, and left Miss Sophy drinking the morning chocolate that Aggie had brought for Beth. In Miss Sophy's bag, she had hardly been surprised to find a heavy purse. Goodness knew where that had come from. For, as much as the general kept his ward liberally supplied with pin money, he would hardly give her this sum. But it did not surprise her. Young and naive Sophy certainly was, but she was certain to make plans to protect herself. She had once confided to Beth that she kept a hat pin on her person at all times, in case of emergencies. That night at Vauxhall had included one such an emergency, when a gentleman had become over-familiar with her during a waltz, and had tried to take her in one of the shady walks. No hat-pin at the ready, Miss Sophy had stamped forcefully on his instep and he had yelped, but made to catch her again. Beth, observing the start of this from some distance, had run to her and discreetly pushed the gentlemen, still a little unbalanced, to the ground. Beth remembered how they had grasped hands and run off into the trees, Miss Sophy giggling and she herself, from the sheer relief of nerves, had joined her. They had been prostrate with laughter for some time, and this was the charm of Miss Sophy, and the danger. But at least the incident had finally allowed Beth to persuade her to go. For Beth had seen that as the wine flowed the behaviour of some of the revellers was becoming quite shocking. Indeed, since losing her position, that night had haunted Beth's nightmares: full of leering faces, scantily clad ladies and large grasping, wandering hands. Vauxhall Gardens, for all its glittering evening beauty, was like Sodom to her.

Sophy had enquired, casually, 'What time are we to go to the Horescombes' today, if your marquis so desires?'

Beth could see that Miss Sophy was considering her options. Her opinion that the Horescombes had not suffered enough, had deeply concerned Beth. If she were not able to play this part of maid and mistress as she desired (and Beth was so tempted to let her really experience the work under a housekeeper's eagle eye, sleeping in a room that was never heated at all) she was liable to run in some other direction to achieve her aim. So Beth had answered casually, forgiving herself the necessary untruth, 'Oh, in the afternoon. The princess wants to walk in the park after breakfast. I have not wanted to go since I saw Miss Oaksett on the first day.'

'Jane? Did you really? What did she say to you?' said Sophy, rapt.

'It is quite alright, she did not recognise me at all.'

'How strange. I suppose she saw you most days for some weeks.'

Beth was not so surprised at her invisibility, but did not answer. 'But today, with you, we can walk at will if we keep our heads down. If the princess is greeted by friends, we may walk on a little, and she will not give my name. It will not be wondered at if I walk with my maid. It will give you a chance to play your rôle to perfection.'

'How amusing. I shall be in the hall, with your bonnet and pelisse, just like the perfect lady's maid, in an hour.'

'I must to breakfast.'

'What about mine? I was told to be in the kitchen for six o'clock.'

'You will not be fed if you missed it.'

'I am becoming rather tired of being a lady's maid,' Miss Sophy said.

Beth went down to breakfast, and was pleased to note the marquis's absence. He was desperately disappointed in her, she knew. He wanted her to confide, but he would soon find why she could not. Emmi made a bright and talkative breakfast companion, avoiding all mention of today's errand. Beth knew her intention was to console, and she tried to conceal her own heart.

As soon they were in the hall, where Miss Sophy stood pert and upright, holding her pelisse and bonnet, next to Cécile who was holding Emmi's.

Beth and the Mistaken Identity

They put them on, and Beth looked away from Miss Sophy's dancing eyes to Dobson's, who nodded. The plan was in action. They moved to the carriage, and a footman opened the door, where the marquis was discovered inside. As Emmi mounted, Beth saw Sophy's eyes dart to the footman who had appeared with her and Beth's bags, and was securing them onto the back with leather straps. She looked at Beth, who met her gaze squarely.

'Where are we going?' she said in an urgent whisper.

'Horescombe House,' Beth answered.

'How *dare* you?' But she wasted no more time on words and grasped at her skirts, whirling around. The tall figure of Frost blocked her path. She tried to move around him, but he moved too, and when she twirled in the other direction, she found another large figure block her path.

'You may as well get in,' said Beth quietly.

'I shall tell them!' hissed Sophy.

'Do. All will be known in ten minutes at any rate.'

'*Why?*'

'Because the Horescombes do not deserve to worry for you one more moment. You affect them more than you know.'

Sophy shot a furious look at her, but entered the carriage. It was a silent journey to Horescombe House.

The old timbered building was a triangular

oasis in the new London. There was even a drive, and they drove down it, the tension mounting.

They got down and the marquis, his face grim, pulled at the old bell by the tall oak doors, and they all four waited.

Suddenly Beth broke the silence. 'No!' she said to herself, 'It must be me.' She turned to Wrexham, who stood stiff and pale and said, grasping his arm so that he looked at her. 'It is she who is Sophy Ludgate, and I who am the maid.'

He froze and she heard Emmi gasp. The door opened and she was glad.

Chapter 14

After a brief, devastated glance at Emmi, Wrexham made his way inside with the party as though in a dream. They were shown into a fine old room, with the enormous fireplace alight at this early hour. The general was not present, only Lady Ernestine, wearing an odd dress made of poplin, as though she were about to garden, and two other older ladies he did not recognise. They were perhaps in their forties, and one had dark brows and a fierce energy about her, while the other, with a fluttering hand and an ever moving glance reminded him of his mother's cousin, Cynthia, who only waited for the next blow to befall her, and annoyingly sought to please him to an excess. He was still reeling from shock, but he took all this in in a second. The maid, or Miss Ludgate, moved forward to Lady Ernestine, but her ladyship patently ignored her, choosing instead to greet him and his sister with her mannish handshake and simple apologies for the aggravation he had been put to. Wrexham supposed he said what was wanted in reply, he hardly knew.

Then she turned to Beth, who stood stiffly, with her eyes down. 'Thank you so much for your note last evening, Beth, it relieved our minds of too much care.'

'Traitor!' said Sophy Ludgate, with a dark look at Beth.

Wrexham wondered if on the ride, he had guessed something of this. The carriage was full of the energy of the maid's repressed fury, and there was something in the superior tilt of her chin as she kept her gaze out of the window, that was not the behaviour of a maid. He had felt from the first that there was a mystery about her, but he had been blind to the mystery of Beth.

Lady Ernestine rounded on her. 'Enough! I do not wish to hear your voice until I give you leave.'

The harshness of her ladyship's tone had its effect, Sophy Ludgate stepped back, but still fulminating. Lady Ernestine picked up a folded and sealed missive and gave it into Beth's hand. She took it, dazed and unheeding, but her eyes fixed on Lady Ernestine's face as though to an anchor.

'When Miss Fosdyke told me you had lost your position doing Sophy's bidding, I was most grieved. Perhaps you *should* have told her ladyship about that dreadful outing, but —'

Beth interrupted, rather unlike a maid, Wrexham thought — but numbly. 'I was afraid if I told, she would make an assignation another night and

Beth and the Mistaken Identity

I might not be there to aid her.'

'But Beth,' objected Sophy, touching her sleeve, 'I quite thought you loved our adventure at Vauxhall Gardens. I dressed you up, and you became a lady for the night and danced and everything! Why, I find you most ungrateful.'

'Enjoy it?' said Beth, her tongue spurned. '*Enjoy* straining to see you every moment, heading off rakes and worse, worrying every minute if you would be recognised—'

'She was!' his sister informed them. Everyone looked at Emmi, shocked. 'But it's Vauxhall, you know,' she continued, waving an airy hand, 'you can always claim it was a mistaken identity. The whole world is intoxicated, anyway.'

Lady Ernestine looked grim. Then she turned back to Beth. 'You were right, my girl, that Sophy would have found a way. I never met a more determined person in my life.' The Ludgate girl looked proud at this and Wrexham looked at the two sisters, one who was regarding this with a cool gaze, the other anxiously. 'That letter contains a recommendation from me,' continued Lady Ernestine, still addressing Beth. 'I have worded it to suggest that you were *my* lady's maid, referred to you as Culpepper, you know, and have written on paper with Grandpapa's crest. I believe you may seek a higher position *now* than that which you held.'

'Culpepper!' hissed Emmi at his side, but he hardly heard.

His emotions, which had frozen since Beth's announcement, were beginning to come crashing upon him, and he wished to cast the chairs about the room and scream to the heavens in his frustration. He looked at her, that lovely face — and his sense of betrayal overcame him. She *had* told them — but two seconds before they got here was hardly sufficient. How would he have reacted to her had she told him before? At the inn? When they reached London? Last night? He hardly knew, so much in a tumult was he. She was answering her ladyship.

'I hardly deserve your kindness,' he saw a tear fall on her cheek and had the urge to wipe it away. Why was he still—? His hands were already in fists, and he gripped them tighter.

The general had entered the room. His tall frame still moved in a soldier's walk, but his military-whiskered face was dangerously high in colour. As he glared in Miss Ludgate's direction, it became higher still. He approached Wrexham.

'I must apologise, Wrexham, Your Highness, that I was not here to greet you.' They exchanged bows. 'But this matter has tried me to the utmost, and my doctor sent me a cursed draught, as I have been overwrought. My ward missing, and with no chaperone. She normally has that at least. But I could not find that any maid was missing from the house where we were.' In all this time, he did not look again at Sophy Ludgate, and Wrexham felt he could not yet, in case his blood exploded.

'It is quite true, I am usually very careful, no matter what you think,' answered the pert little person, who in Wrexham's opinion had been too often spared the rod in her childhood. He would be willing to make up for that deficit now. 'But I could not persuade the maid to come.'

Lord Horescombe eventually turned his eye on her, and had to breathe heavily as he did so. '*And,*' said the general, 'you are guilty of theft.' His tone of admonishment dropped a little as he added, 'It was dashed awkward at the first stop. Miss Fosdyke had to pay for the refreshments.'

'As though that could possibly repay you for—' twittered one of the ladies behind.

But she stopped abruptly, and Wrexham feared she had been nipped by her sister.

Sophy Ludgate gurgled at this, but was quelled by her guardian's awful eye. 'But sir,' she said, putting one pretty hand on his arm consolingly, 'you must perceive that I needed funds in case of emergency. You always say that the success of any campaign is preparation. You would not want me to be *stranded* somewhere, with perhaps some ruffians nearby, without the funds to hire a carriage?'

'Well, no,' conceded the general, 'but—'

This was Sophy Ludgate's particular genius, Wrexham suddenly saw, to make her outrageous behaviour seem reasonable, and to make her listener collude with her, as the general had, so that they end up almost approving it. Beth had no doubt been subjected to a great deal of her affection, then her self-serving logic.

'And I was to bring the purse back to you directly, for I really *meant* to return to Horescombe House yesterday. Only it was the drollest thing. I met a servant who mistook me for Sophy Ludgate's maid! I knew almost at once that it must be Beth, who was pursuing her own masquerade.'

He heard Beth gasp but could not see her face.

'Did you really take your mistress's identity?' said the general, shocked. 'How came you to live in Wrexham's home?'

Beth's head was cast down, and her fingers clasped.

Emmi stepped forward. 'Beth never did claim to be Miss Ludgate, your lordship, I assure you. Indeed she denied it always. But I believed I recognised her as a girl I saw at Vauxhall Gardens, whom someone told me was Miss Sophy Ludgate.'

'The whole town will be talking of her!' The old man grasped at his cravat.

'Oh, that will pass,' consoled Emmi, 'But the point is, we would not let Beth go until you returned.'

'Well, it is very odd,' said the general, 'and not at all the thing. You should have spoken truly, Beth, and remembered your position.'

'I tried, but I feared—' uttered Beth in a small voice. 'At first, I did not have many shillings for travel—'

'Do you mean to tell me that Lady Foster let you go without your wages?' demanded Lady Ernestine.

'She said I should have them, *perhaps,* at the end of the quarter.'

'That woman!' said Ernestine disgustedly.

'So selfishly, I took the offered transport to London, thinking to seek a position at an inn.'

'*That's* why you were there, at that inn,' Wrexham said, addressing her for the first time. 'You were seeking a position.'

'Yes.' Beth answered, but she did not look at him.

He remembered Tennant's behaviour with the serving girl. 'I can imagine why you decided against it.' She met his eyes fleetingly for a moment and dropped them again. He wanted — but he stopped himself moving to her.

'But then,' said Emmi, 'we wouldn't let you go.'

Beth said nothing.

'And by that time, I suppose you needed someone to explain *why* you found yourself in such a position, someone to explain *Sophy* to them,' said Lady Ernestine frankly.

'I think you are all spending a great deal of time on Beth and none on me at all,' said the pert little miss.

The general turned to her. 'Do not worry, miss, I will get to you in a moment.' Then he reached into his pocket and took out a packet, which he held out to Beth. 'You deserve this reward, my dear, for the unjust treatment you have received, only for being appointed maid to the most headstrong little termagant that God every created.' Beth let the packet drop into her hand.

'Thirty pieces of silver!' hissed Sophy. 'You *betrayed* me today—'

But her words were cut off by a stentorian voice.

'You will apologise to Beth at once, Sophy!' The voice fairly cut through the room, stunning them all. Miss Fosdyke, of the dark brows, came forward then — and even in her old gown she looked regal in a way his sister could not quite match. 'At once!' Her voice rose again, and Sophy almost jumped. For the first time she was shame-faced and she said, 'I apologise, Beth.'

'And you may apologise to my sister, too, who spent the whole of yesterday's journey crying, worrying herself about you. I did not give myself the trouble, for everything I have learnt about the most selfish individual of my acquaintance told me you would look after yourself, even if no other person concerns you!'

Sophy, still shaken, said, turning to the younger sister, 'I'm sorry Miss Wilhelmina. But it isn't true what your sister says. I had laid my plans the night you came to me in my room, and I delayed *two whole days more* because I knew how much you were enjoying that dreadful party!'

Miss Fosdyke cast her eyes to heaven. 'I apologise, your lordship,' she said, turning to the general, 'it was not my place to speak.'

'Nonsense! You are family after all, and I could not have expressed it better myself.' He suddenly

Beth and the Mistaken Identity

looked at Beth. 'You may go,' he dismissed her, 'and fare thee well.'

Wrexham saw Beth headed for the door and he leapt forward in his imagination to her going into the street, strong and upright in her blue pelisse, and disappearing from his life forever. 'No!' he ordered, 'She will stay!' He turned to the general whose eyebrows had risen, 'With your permission, sir.' But his voice was not pleading, and the general held his gaze for a moment. Wrexham met his squarely. The general nodded finally, and Beth took up that rigid position she had adopted, off to one side. He did not know what he was thinking, what his complex and turbulent feelings were. But he needed her in his sight.

'You, young lady, will stay in this house under our eye, for the foreseeable future. I have asked the kind ladies to stay and they have obliged me by saying yes, even though you have caused them so much distress. One of us shall be beside you at all times — and at night I shall have you tied to your bed if need be.' Wrexham saw Sophy look at a work table beside the fireplace, where a piece of linen was stitched with colourful silks. She looked contrite however, and the general continued. 'I cannot conceive of why you behave this way Sophy. It is beyond me. You disobey us every turn—is it to meet some swains, to flirt with men to bolster your self-esteem? Or to choose your own husband without our help? This is dangerous indeed!'

Sophy flushed brightly, but it was Beth's voice who said, 'No, your lordship. Excuse me, but you are much mistaken.'

'Well, Beth,' said Lady Ernestine practically, after a moment of shock that Beth would put herself forward so. 'Explain her to us. You have been most often in her company this last year.'

Beth came forward a little, still with a maid's demeanour, and said. 'It is not the *gentlemen* Miss Sophy likes, but the *adventure*. I was worried a little by the male attention she received, indeed *invited* sometimes, with her winning ways. But she was never interested in *them,* only how they could further her plans. She is really very innocent in her dealing with gentlemen, I think, and cannot conceive why her friends are sometimes cast into transports at a smile, or cast down by a gentleman failing to dance with them. Miss Sophy cares for none of that.' The general looked somewhat reassured by that, Wrexham could not help noticing. 'Our trip to Vauxhall was not to flirt or be flirted with, although because Miss Sophy is so pretty it is inevitable that she was pursued. It was for the spectacle, the experience, and also because she was forbidden.'

'Contrary eh? Just wants to flout us. When I had such soldiers in the ranks, I had them birched!'

'But Miss Sophy was not made to be a soldier, but a general, like *you* sir,' said Beth.

Here she was, in the quiet little voice of a maid, defending the creature who had almost destroyed her. How like her, Wrexham thought. She had not finished.

'Do you know what I saw sir, when you were threatening to tie her down? Her eyes went to the scissors on that sewing table, already planning an escape from a punishment I know you did not really mean.'

'You are most observant for a maid,' said the general a little gruffly.

Wrexham could see her think it then: *How do you know what a servant observes, you never ask?*

'I do not think you will ever best her in the way you wish. She has a determined spirit and a creative mind, and a desire to experience everything that she may.'

There was a pause, everyone but Emmeline and he amazed that Beth had spoken so.

Lady Ernestine said reasonably, 'All you say rings true to me. But if she is not to make some husband's life a misery, her wilfulness must be curbed.'

'But I do not want a husband!' broke in Sophy. 'They seem to me the most useless thing imaginable.' She seemed to consider, 'Unless I married someone weak enough to do my bidding. I suppose that might work.'

Miss Wilhelmina gave a horrified gasp. 'To be wed when there is no affection...'

Her sister sniffed. 'Do not fear, my dear sister, Sophy has enough affection for herself to last a lifetime.'

Even Lady Ernestine seemed shocked at Sophy's marriage plans, and Wrexham could not blame her. Of all the heartless little jades ...! Lady Ernestine turned to Beth and said, 'Well, since you have given us her character so wisely, Beth, how would *you* tame Sophy?'

General Lord Horescombe expostulated, but indecipherably, perhaps at her ladyship's asking help of a junior servant.

Beth seemed, for once, at a loss. 'I do not know, your ladyship, I only know your current plan is not to the purpose.'

Wrexham moved forward a little. 'If I might venture a suggestion, your ladyship?' He was nearer to Beth now, and though there was an arm's length between them, he felt the frisson that went through her, and the heat in him. They did not look at each other.

Lady Ernestine shrugged. 'Continue on, Wrexham, all our dirty linen has been washed before you, after all.'

'I do not see why you are all talking about me as if I were a prob—' said Sophy petulantly.

Wrexham ignored her. 'What I think might be helpful is to go along with her nature,' the general barked an objection, but Wrexham held up his hand. 'Not her wilfulness, but her love of new experience. You might do what your papa did with you when you were a young buck, sir, anxious to stretch your legs.'

'The Grand Tour? But she is a *lady*.'

Beth and the Mistaken Identity

Wrexham forbore to question this description of Miss Ludgate, but it cost him something. 'Yes, but just as wild as you were, perhaps. My generation were not able to enjoy such an experience as The Grand Tour, and my own visit to Europe,' he said dryly, talking of his time in the Peninsular War, 'was less than felicitous. But my father regretted that I did not have that experience.'

'It made a man of me!' agreed the general gruffly, 'but not for a lady, I say!'

'Well,' Lady Ernestine said, considering, 'since the monster has been tamed, I have been wishing to visit certain bookshops in Italy, and another in Amsterdam, that I hear have many treasures I have been looking for,' Lady Ernestine said, considering.

Sophy whirled and hugged her, 'Oh, Lady Ernestine, do you mean it? To travel and see Europe! It has always been my dream. I was determined, when once I inherited, to go with a companion to Europe. But I hardly knew if I could wait until my majority. Six years!'

'On your own, with only another lady?' gasped Miss Wilhelmina.

'Oh no, I should have chosen two tall strong footmen, perhaps, and a groom and a coachman, and I would buy a pistol, you know, in case of bandits.'

'Foolhardy to the last,' said Miss Fosdyke, disgusted.

Sophy turned to Beth, and ran to her arms. 'It is

all your doing, Beth. You explained it all as I could not. I am sorry I was foul to you, but you *did* betray me.'

Beth looked and he saw exasperation and affection in her eyes, in equal measure.

'*I* have not said it will be so, miss,' said the general.

'But we all know sir that Lady Ernestine's word is law,' replied Sophy in a teasing tone, using her charming eyes to good effect.

The old man sighed heavily. 'Well, if Miss Fosdyke and her sister will accompany us ...'

'Europe, sister!' said Miss Wilhelmina, with a hand to her bosom.

Miss Fosdyke looked unmoved.

'Between all of us, we shall stop you running off with some swarthy Italian artist,' said the general, defeated.

'That's all settled,' said Emmi, suddenly entering the fray. 'And now — Wrexham?'

With Beth so near, and trembling at his proximity, it was suddenly blindingly clear to him. He turned to her, and tilted her face towards his. 'May I have the very great pleasure of asking you to be my wife?' he said, simply.

The general, who had been accepting the ecstatic hugs of his ward, turned and said, shocked, 'Who, Sophy?'

'No,' said Wrexham, eyes still on Beth. 'Miss Culpepper.'

'The *maid*?

'Yes,' he replied calmly.

'You must have taken leave of your senses, my boy. Think what you owe to your name...'

Beth ran from the room, and Wrexham followed her determinedly.

Chapter 15

He caught her arm before she had time to cross the old hall, and Beth cried out.

'In here,' ordered Wrexham shortly, opening a door.

She held her tears back and straightened, she would be obedient, of course. It was her place. She thrust away the thing he had said in the other room, knew it must be some dreadful jest, knew she must take refuge in her position. 'Yes, my lord.' And she walked through the library door, past him, very much in the manner of an obedient maid. She got to the centre of the room before she felt him turn her around, and in a second, she was in his arms, the hard kiss a punishment and a promise. Two seconds later, her arms were wrapped around his neck, and she was pulling him closer in a desperate attempt to have what she had longed for so long. It was as though they melded together, as though, she thought, they moved to a higher place, somewhere where it was permitted, even natural, to be his. She felt him give himself to

Beth and the Mistaken Identity

her and she offered herself to him as the kiss became more desperate, for what she did not know. It lasted too long and it was too explosive and she wrenched herself away.

'No, oh no!' she said in a whisper, standing back from him and turning her head.

The marquis stood back too, she had just glimpsed the fire still in his eyes, looking at her determinedly. 'Yes,' he answered simply, and then he pulled her to him again, so that she fell into his arms, accepting the hot kisses on her neck and face, trying to pull some part of her away from him, but merging with him instead. They must not. She pulled away again. Gesturing to him to stay away, bright tears in her eyes, threatening to fall.

He stood back, and once he had controlled his breathing, he said, 'I hardly know what I feel about today, about the huge deception you perpetrated. You let me get close to you, you must have known —'

'How could I think you would care for me?' She looked at him, desperately apologetic. 'I only wanted to escape at first, but then the Horescombes were to return — and well, I hoped it would give me a way to explain about what I had already done — but I never thought I could cause you pain. Anger, yes, but not pain.'

'Oh, I am angry, I am furious with you, and shocked and questioning how I could ever have let this happen, but as I stood in there, watching you,

I could not change one thing. I want you, Beth.'

Beth's tears fell, as she looked at him in penitence.

'And I love you,' she said simply. Her eyes filled, obscuring his face. 'I could not deny it if I would. You know it now.' He took a step forward, but she halted him with a gesture. 'But now you are doing to me what I have feared since I was turned off.' She looked at him piteously. '*Please* do not, Wrexham, for I cannot resist you. Whatever style you set me up in, whatever jewels and carriages you give me, it will be the start of my slide downward. When you are finished with me there will be another man, not so rich, and then I shall either end my life in poverty, or on the streets.' He was silent, but she thought he remembered some women he had treated thus, perhaps not really facing the truth since he was the first or second keeper, who sent her off with coin, and who had not had to consider her eventual fate. Some women might retire to the country, she thought, but not all, and she thought she saw that knowledge in his eyes in a split second. 'Perhaps you would pension me off, but I would have lost my honour, and I could hardly live with how far I had fallen from the will of God.' She paced the room, to be further from him. 'All I ever wanted was to be a respectable girl, to do my best in my position, and rise, perhaps. And to stay away from such temptations as this.'

Wrexham, who had held his tongue in check with difficulty, now spoke, frustrated. 'Beth, I

Beth and the Mistaken Identity

asked you to become my wife, my marchioness, not to be my mistress.'

She turned on him, impassioned. 'Do you think I could *love* you and ever let you do that?'

'My will, my choice Beth.' She shook her head dismissively. Now it was his turn to pace, then he stopped, turning to her. 'Do you know that in Wrexham Lodge there is a picture of my great-great-grandmother in milkmaid's dress? Shall I tell you why?'

'It was a fashion of the time to paint ladies in pastoral scenes. There was a portrait in Foster Hall of a previous Lady Foster in costume herding goats.' Beth was confused by this deviation, and answered vaguely.

'No. It was because she *was* a milkmaid. My great-great-grandfather fell in love with her and took her to wife. And when my father told me the tale he said,' Wrexham adopted a rough baritone voice, that she assumed must be his father's, '*Every few generations, we're in want of new blood. Only that's no excuse to marry an opera dancer.*'

Beth laughed at this a little. 'Not nowadays, Wrexham, the *ton* would never accept me, and they would blame *you* for my presence. And Emmi, too — we cannot hurt her so! No, Wrexham, you have been overturned, as I have, by a few days dalliance, and you will recover.' Her voice broke as she said it.

He didn't drop his eye. 'I have never met a woman like you, Beth, and I never will again. I cannot give you up, whatever the cost.'

'Then you will ask me to be your mistress, and I will say yes. But I beg you, for the sake of my honour, not to do so. I need you to be stronger than me, Wrexham. I am just a maid, who tricked a marquis. You do not think so now, but you will forget me.'

The air was still and Wrexham sought for an answer.

The door opened and the princess entered at this time, before Wrexham had time to move. Emmi looked from one to the other, and came to Beth, saying. 'All I could think when I heard the truth is that I may have turned you out if you had spoken more plainly that first night.'

'I should not have—'

'I don't know how to feel about that, still.'

'I am so sorry...'

'But I do know that if I had, I should have missed having the best friend of my life.'

'Your Royal Highness,' Beth curtsied, 'I hardly know what to say—' but the princess had thrown herself around Beth's neck, before she completed the curtsy, and Beth held her, crying on her shoulder.

The princess withdrew for a moment. 'Beth, do you say your name is Culpepper?'

'Yes,' said Beth, a trifle dully, nursing the ache in her heart. It was so like Emmi to forgive her, and she did not deserve it. And, she thought insanely, her nose must be red-tipped by now. Soon all her

Beth and the Mistaken Identity

dignity would be gone. She *must* leave soon.

'It is an old name,' Wrexham said, and Emmi turned to him directly.

'Yes, that's what I thought, Toby. Kent is full of old Culpepper estates, of one branch or another.' She turned back to Beth who was feeling dazed and hardly paying attention to this, her head and heart warring over the things he'd said to her. The joy of him loving her, enough to ruin his life, was fighting with her agony of the inevitable parting. The princess said something to her, and she missed it, and she excused herself. '*I said*, do you know the present Lord Culpepper?'

'No, 'said Beth answering automatically, 'I have never met him, but according to my father and the family bible, he shared a great-grandfather with my father.' Beth looked embarrassed. 'Before my father died, when he was — intoxicated — he often talked about how if it wasn't for primy-jenchoor we would live on a big estate.'

'Primogeniture,' said the marquis. Beth looked a question. 'The eldest son inherits.'

'My great-great-grandfather was a second son who was cast off by his family — probably for being a wastrel by all accounts — with only enough to buy a farm. He wasn't fit for it, and ran it into the ground. His son sold it and then rented it back and became a tenant-farmer. In due course, my father took it on, but I fear he was no better farmer than his father or grandfather before him. But his connection to the aristocracy meant that he allowed my mother to teach us our letters. She had been a lady's maid in a fine house, you know, so she could read and write well. He always said, though we never heeded him, that if enough people died, we might inherit again.' The others were looking at her closely. 'But you must understand that my late father, though it is disrespectful to say so, was a ranting fool at some times.'

'That's it, Toby!'

'Culpepper must be made to recognise her as his relative.'

Beth interrupted. 'Lord Culpepper rejected my father many years ago,' said Beth, hardly understanding what they were about. Emmi and Wrexham were fully concentrated on each other now, not minding her at all.

'His lordship is a stiff-rumped old ox — how will you manage it, Toby?'

'I will manage it, have no fear,' the marquis said dangerously.

'And then you could have met Beth at Culpepper's estate—' Emmi frowned. 'Though who would believe you would ever go *there*?'

'Booth goes shooting there, I accompanied him.'

'*That* might work. And then Beth was visiting, as a family member, and you met her and fell in love. It is perfect!'

The sister and brother looked at each other, pleased with themselves. Beth was exasperated.

'You are forgetting that I have a family. Do you expect me just to abandon them because they might be an embarrassment?'

Emmi turned, with a bright smile on her face, and a careless shrug. 'Oh, that is quite easy, Beth. Toby will buy them some large farming estate and they can oversee the workers. There are any number of gentleman farmers in town, you know. And if your family are a little lax in their manners, your mother may change that, now that she has the leisure. I expect that she has an excellent grasp of manners and so on from her former position.' She grasped Beth's hands. 'How large *is* your family, Beth? How many brothers and sisters do you have?'

'Three brothers and two sisters.' Beth answered distractedly. What did this mean?

'You must tell me all about them later. They can visit town in a year or so, once they have become accustomed to their new status.'

Beth's head was reeling, but she saw so many things at once that it was hard to keep up. Her sister Nessie didn't have to go into service, her mother respectable and comfortable, the children reared to a better life. She knew Jem might resist gentrification, but he would go along for his mother's comfort, and he would welcome the scope of a larger farm. Emmi and Wrexham were continuing with plans that made her breathless.

'But what will Beth do until the wedding?' Emmi said, turning to Wrexham again. 'It might not be politic to take her home with us, much as I'd like to. No need to stir gossip. She will be enough of a surprise to the polite world.'

'I will get a special licence and marry her within the week. I just need her mother's signature.'

Beth squeaked.

Emmi grew thoughtful, 'No, that won't do Toby, there must be no hint of the irregular. I am sure the general would permit her to remain here, on another footing, of course.'

'I—' Beth interjected. They ignored her.

'In a house where she was once a maid? It would be most uncomfortable for her. No, I may require her to live at Culpepper's address.'

'Beth live with that sour old stick? I won't allow it!' Emmi declared. Dear Emmi, how could she still care for her? But they were both being—

'What else—?' Wrexham replied frowning, and neither of them were looking at Beth. She was beginning to be amused.

'I have it!' said Emmi after a moment. 'A Culpepper cousin! Miss Daphne Culpepper, who did not take in town, now lives with the old man in perfect misery, says Lady Austen. She told me to be especially kind to her if we meet at the subscription library, or in the park, and so I am!' said Emmi in a saintly tone. 'What is more natural in that a young lady visit the home of her fiancé accompanied by *family*?'

'Yes, and the general and Lady Ernestine will recognise her, I'm sure. And I shall stay Tennant's mouth about the first time we met.' He turned to Beth, 'You see Beth? What you feared would hurt

Beth and the Mistaken Identity

me, will not do so at all. Now you *must* marry me.'

Beth smiled at them both, but looked at him sadly.

'I cannot.'

Emmi looked aghast, and Wrexham grim. The princess moved to Beth and kissed her. 'I need my friend *about* me, Beth.' Beth smiled weakly, 'And now I will leave you, and trust to Toby's fabled powers of persuasion.' She turned and left the room, with a last look at her brother.

He strode to her. 'Why? Do you not *wish* to be my wife?'

'Not your marchioness, I am not *fit*. Even if the Culpeppers are persuaded to recognise me, I am still a maid. I pretended otherwise for a few days, but it will not do.'

He took her tiny hand and kissed it, and led her to an ancient settle, taking up her other hand, too. She was breathing heavily. 'I do not understand, Beth. You will have to explain to me,' he said gently. But she thought he looked dangerous a little, determined.

She took a deeper breath. 'As a maid, I was content and proud of my position, and of my work. I never dwelt on the inequalities, the world was that way, and I knew myself to be fortunate.' His eyes were on hers, fully attentive. 'But from the first of being mistaken for a lady, I experienced a different sensibility. I saw and felt every casual slight to the maids made, every problem in the household, and I was wounded and stirred to feel the injustice of it. How can I be a marchioness, and rule over the staff, and treat others as I would not wish to be treated — I could not.'

'Do you want me to cast off all my servants, Beth?' Wrexham asked. 'To do my own laundry?'

She laughed. 'I should like to see you try,' she said, thinking of laundry day at Foster Hall. 'Of course I do not — and leave so many without a position? No, but I cannot join you in this.'

He looked at her face, and took another tack. 'What is it you wanted, Beth, as a servant?'

'A stable household. Being fed and sheltered and to have some money to send to my mother. And I had all that. But there were the slights, or the impossible demands —'

'Impossible?'

Make this dress by tomorrow; have dinner sent up in ten minutes, those kind of things. But it was part of my position and I grew to cope with it. My failure was in coping with Miss Sophy.'

'You failed to keep yourself safe, while you aided her, though she could never be brought to acknowledge it.' He smiled at her in a way that weakened her resolve. She saw those blue, enticing eyes and she almost pulled away in desperation. But he became serious, still holding her hands in a way that thrilled, but kept her captive. 'But now, I beg you. Help me be a better master, Beth. Help me know what my household needs, and how I can change things, as you already started. Tell me when I am cruel or unthinking to

Beth and the Mistaken Identity

those beneath me. I assure you, my father raised me to be respectful of my dependants. If I fall short, I will have you at my side to change me.'

'How could I bear to be decked in satins and silk while others starve?'

'I *shall* have you decked in silks, my Beth. Think of it as the garments for your new position. We two cannot change the world. And in truth, before I met you, I would not even have wished to. I wished to be fair, but not generous. But you have alerted me to many things, even before this day. And together we can change many things.' She shook her head and looked down, trying to stop herself from dreaming it possible. He gave her hands a squeeze to make her look up again. 'I went to a lecture the week before we met, and I heard a young fellow named Elfoy talk of the managements of estates. The Earl of Grandiston is his friend and mine, and Grandiston insisted I attend, and that I would hear an amazing story. I did, Beth. His wife had inherited a rundown estate, and with no money to help her, she and he have made improvements to the land and begun to make it a great estate once more. They employed returned soldiers, many of whom were injured, and had fallen on hard times.'

'It is an affront that men who fought for us should fall so low,' she found herself saying hotly, for her brother had almost joined Wellington's Army, perhaps as a boy-drummer, had not their father suddenly died.

'Yes, and many such were my own men, and of course I have given to relief funds. But what the Elfoys have achieved is far in advance of this. He said, and I was moved by it, that you only have to offer a man food, shelter and hope, and he will give you his all.'

'Ah, that is quite beautiful.'

'It is. And I have many estates in which I could employ his methods. If you marry me, Beth, we could do it together.'

Beth glowed at him and her fingers were burning with his touch. 'Oh, Wrexham, if only — I do not deserve—'

'I have bribed and cajoled you Beth, and let me tell you that many young ladies would have accepted me with the merest request,' he was smiling and teasing her as usual, and she smiled a little, too. Then his expression changed. 'But that is *all*.' His cleft chin was set, and he looked dangerous and breath-taking. He pulled her to him, and kissed her roughly. Then he pulled away, laughing, but adding in a instructive tone, 'It is clear that for the sake of many starving families, you have no choice but to marry me.'

Beth was trembling now, and smiling her broadest smile. 'I do not think I will marry you for that reason, my lord.' She kissed him again, this time tender and giving. 'I think I will marry you because I love you very much.' Then she had a thought. 'And, of course for the sake of the future Agamemnon.'

He laughed, and held her closer, making her tremble anew.

They continued in this happy way until interrupted by Sophy Ludgate and the princess barging in without knocking. Beth pulled away, flushed.

'I could not stop her!' apologised Emmi.

'Beth,' Sophy began, 'I have just been saying to Lady Ernestine that it would be much more suitable, besides cheaper, if *you* were to accompany us to Europe instead of the Misses Fosdyke. You know we will have such fun.'

Beth visibly shuddered at the thought. 'And deprive Miss Wilhelmina of her chance at travel? I could not.' Sophy began to look familiarly mulish at her will being thwarted. 'In any case, I shall be at home, busy being a marchioness.' She took Wrexham's hand, and looked at him lovingly.

Emmi squealed, 'I knew it!' she ran over and dragged both of them to their feet, and hugged them both at once, in a less than regal fashion.

'Let us leave, Beth. We are going home.'

'Well,' said Sophy Ludgate, disgusted, 'When we might have been merry together!' And she tossed her curls and left the room.

'Do you know, I am quite glad we got the wrong Sophy Ludgate, for I do not at all care for that girl,' said Wrexham, tucking both ladies' hands into his bent elbows in a joyous and gallant fashion. 'Thank goodness for the Mistaken Identity.'

Beth smiled at him, and at her friend on his arm, and joined them in going back to the great house that would soon, amazingly, serve as her home. How she loved him now, and how she would strive to make him never regret his decision. She looked at Emmi, so very pleased with herself and all her Culpepper plots. But Beth knew that both she and her blue-eyed Marquis of Wrexham would have striven to keep her whatever her name had been. Just because of who they were. The dearest friends of her life. She would never have allowed it of course, but as she looked at the set of Wrexham's chin, she knew he would have pursued her, wherever she had run to.

'Well, I shall have no shopping to speak of at dinner tonight,' said Emmi merrily, 'Whatever shall we have to talk of?'

'Should I go to sleep at my club?' asked Wrexham, frowning.

'Oh, no! We've had guests refused entry since Beth arrived. No one need know she is there 'til Miss Culpepper arrives.' The princess smiled. 'We shall just have another dinner together as usual. And tomorrow after you have seen old Culpepper, I can go and spread the word of my brother's sudden romance!'

All three left the house, choosing — shockingly — to send a message by a footman that they would make their farewells at another time. They walked towards Grosvenor Square, eschewing the carriage, and Lady Ernestine, watching them from the window, thought them a happy group. She did not approve of marrying out of one's class, as this departure together suggested, but seeing them walk joyously off, she felt that all three had some magical connection that could not be denied.

Everyone else joined her at the window, watching them.

'Well,' huffed Lord Horescombe. I hope Wrexham knows what he's about.'

'I think it is like a fairy tale,' said Miss Wilhelmina, wiping a tear away with a wisp of a handkerchief.

'You *would*,' said Miss Florencia flatly. 'I cannot approve of such an unequal match.' In the distance, she saw Wrexham look down on the little maid, and almost felt his loving gaze even from this distance. A tear rose in her eyes. 'But Beth is a good girl.' Her calm was shaken a little, and she grasped her sister's hand.

Sophy was looking too, still disgruntled at the thwarting of her will. 'Well,' she said a trifle sulkily, 'I suppose I shall have to curtsy deeply to the new Marchioness of Wrexham, when I meet her.'

'I suppose,' said Lady Ernestine with relish, 'that you will indeed.'

Alicia Cameron

Get Alicia's very favourite short(ish) story by joining her newsletter: here or buy it on Amazon for only 99p/99c GetBook.at/Angelique

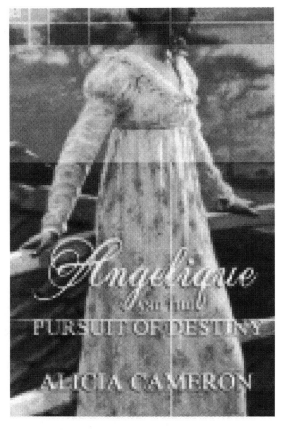

Also by Alicia Cameron:

The Inspirational Edwardian Romance with an 'Unforgettable heroine...' getBook.at/FrancineT

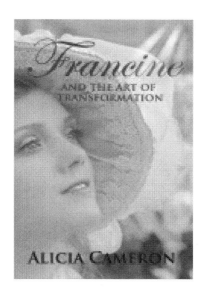

Alicia Cameron

The Regency Romances:

Bestselling Clarissa: GetBook.at/Clarissa
(over 100 Amazon.com reviews)

The Fentons Book 1 and 2:

GetBook.at/Honoria GetBook.at/Felicity

GetBook.at/Delphine

Get an Alicia Cameron Audiobook FREE with a subscription to Audible.

Author's Note:

Dear Lovely Readers,

I can say that now not just in hope, but in the knowledge that I now possess about some of you. I must truly have some of the loveliest readers around. If you have just found this book and like it, please explore my world on https://aliciacameron.co.uk. You can also email me at alicia@aliciacameron.co.uk

Twitter: @aliciaclarissa2
Instagram: aliciaclarissa2
And on Facebook: aliciiacameron.100

I recommend my audiobooks. The majority (including the audio of this book in production at the moment) are read by talented actress Helen Taylor, though I have had Clarissa read by the Heath Miller, a Regency hero in look and gentlemanliness, and a wonderfully fruity reading of Delphine by Rafe Buckley.

I'm entwined in my next world now, an old castle that my reclusive heroine has to makeover for a house party where one of her younger sisters' swains might offer for her.

But the reason that Evangeline did not accept the offers for her hand made to her during her two seasons also arrives. Lord Onslow is deeply in love with another, and he hardly recognises the girl who thinks he was made for her, our heroine Evangeline. She fell in love in a moment, but unfortunately, his attention is still elsewhere.

So far, it is lots of fun. What do you think? Sound promising?

As usual, might I ask you, if you've enjoyed this book, to **LEAVE A REVIEW ON AMAZON?** In order to stop fraud, Amazon has forbidden many fan reviews, and cut down some of my readers' reviews, usually because they've reviewed before. I'm sure it is a glip, but it is frustrating for authors and their fans.

As you are wonderful, take a second to leave a review.

All the very best from my Scottish home to your home,

Alicia

P.S. I'll add a chapter of Book 1 of The Fentons: *Honoria and the Family Obligation*, just to tempt you.

Honoria and the Family Obligation

The Fentons: Book 1

Chapter 1

Blue Slippers

'He has arrived!' said Serena, kneeling on the window seat of their bedchamber. She made a pretty picture there with her sprigged muslin dress foaming around her and one silk stockinged foot still on the floor, but her sister Honoria was too frozen with fear to notice.

'Oh, no,' said Honoria, moving forward in a dull fashion to join her. Her elder brother Benedict had been sitting with one leg draped negligently over the arm of the only comfortable chair in the room and now rose languidly to join his younger sisters. After the season in London, Dickie had begun to ape the manners of Beau Brummel and his cronies, polite, but slightly bored with the world. At one and twenty, it seemed a trifle contrived, even allowing that his long limbs and handsome face put many a town beau to shame.

Serena's dark eyes danced wickedly, 'Here comes the conquest of your triumphant season, your soon-to-be-fiancé.'

Beth and the Mistaken Identity

Dickie grinned, rather more like their childhood companion, 'Your knight in shining armour. If *only* you could remember him.'

'It isn't funny.'

Serena laughed and turned back to the window as she heard the door of the carriage open and the steps let down by Timothy, the one and only footman that Fenton Manor could boast.

'Oh, how did it happen?' Honoria said for the fifteenth time that morning.

Someone in the crowd had said, 'Mr Allison is approaching. But he never dances!' In confusion, she had looked around, and saw the throng around her grow still and part as her hostess approached with a tall gentleman. With all eyes turned to her she stiffened in every sinew. She remembered the voice of Lady Carlisle introducing Mr Allison as a desirable partner, she remembered her mother thrusting her forward as she was frozen with timidity. She remembered his hand lead her to her first waltz of the season. She had turned to her mother for protection as his hand snaked around her waist and had seen that matron grip her hands together and glow with pride. This was Lady Fenton's shining moment, if not her daughter's. Word had it that Mr Allison had danced only thrice this season, each time with his married friends. Lost in the whirl of the dance, she had answered his remarks with single syllables, looking no higher than his chin. A dimpled chin, strong, she remembered vaguely. And though she had previously seen Mr Allison at a distance, the very rich and therefore very interesting Mr Allison, with an estate grander than many a noble-

man, she could not remember more than that he was held to be handsome. (As she told Serena this later, her sister remarked that rich men were very often held to be handsome, strangely related to the size of their purse.)

There was the waltz; there had been a visit to her father in the London house; her mother had informed her of Mr Allison's wishes and that she was to receive his addresses the next afternoon. He certainly visited the next afternoon, and Honoria had been suffered to serve him his tea and her hand had shaken so much that she had kept her eyes on the cup for the rest of the time. He had not proposed, which her mother thought of as a pity, but here she had been saved by Papa, who had thought that Mr Allison should visit them in the country where his daughter and he might be more at their leisure to know each other. 'For she is a little shy with new company and I should wish her perfectly comfortable before she receives your addresses,' Sir Ranalph had told him, as Honoria's mama had explained.

Serena, when told, had thought it a wonderful joke. To be practically engaged to someone you could not remember! She laughed because she trusted to good-natured Papa to save Honoria from the match if it should prove unwanted; her sister had only to say "no".

'Why on earth do you make such a tragedian of yourself, Orry,' had said Serena once Honoria had poured her story out, 'After poor Henrietta Madeley's sad marriage, Papa has always said that to marry with such parental compulsion is scandalously cruel.'

And Honoria had mopped up her tears and felt a

Beth and the Mistaken Identity

good deal better, buoyed by Serena's strength of mind. To be sure, there was the embarrassment to be endured of giving disappointment, but she resolved to do it if Mr Allison's aura of grandeur continued to terrify her.

'And then,' her sister had continued merrily, 'the rich Mr Allison may just turn out to be as handsome as his purse and as good natured as Papa - and you will fall head over heels with him after all.'

The morning after, Honoria had gone for a walk before breakfast, in much better spirits. As she came up the steps to re-enter by the breakfast room, she carelessly caught her new French muslin (fifteen and sixpence the yard, Mama had told her) on the roses that grew on a column. If she took her time and did not pull, she may be able to rescue herself without damage to the dress. She could hear Mama and Papa chatting and gave it no mind until Mama's voice became serious.

'My dear Ranalph, will you not tell me?'

'Shall there be muffins this morning, my dear?' said Papa cheerfully.

'You did not finish your mutton last night and you are falsely cheerful this morning. Tell me, my love.'

'You should apply for a position at Bow Street, my dear. Nothing escapes you.' She heard the sound of an embrace.

'Diversionary tactics, sir, are futile.'

Honoria knew she should not be privy to this, but she was still detaching her dress, thorn by thorn. It was incumbent on her to make a noise, so that they might know she was there, but as she decided to do so, she was frozen by Papa's next words.

'Mr Allison's visit will resolve all, I'm sure.'

Honoria closed her mouth, automatically continuing to silently pluck her dress from the rose bush, anxious to be away.

'Resolve what, dearest?' Honoria could picture her mama on Papa's knee.

'Well, there have been extra expenses – from the Brighton property.' Honoria knew that this was where her uncle Wilbert lived, her father's younger brother. (Dickie had explained that he was a friend of the Prince Regent, which sounded so well to the girls, but Dickie had shaken his head loftily. 'You girls know nothing. Unless you are as rich as a Maharajah, it's ruinous to be part of that set.')

Her father continued, 'Now, now. All is well. If things do not take with Mr Allison, we shall just have to cut our cloth a little, Madame.' He breathed. 'But, Cynthia, I'm afraid another London Season is not to be thought of.'

Honoria felt instant guilt. Her own season had been at a rather later age than that of her more prosperous friends, and she had not been able to understand why Serena and she could not have had it together, for they borrowed each other's clothes all the time. Serena's intrepid spirit would have buoyed hers too and made her laugh, and would have surely helped with her crippling timidity. But when she had seen how many dresses had been required - one day alone she had changed from morning gown to carriage dress to luncheon half dress, then riding habit and finally evening dress. And with so many of the same people at balls, one could not make do - Mama had insisted on twenty evening gowns as the bare minimum. However

Beth and the Mistaken Identity

doughty with a needle the sisters might be, this was beyond their scope, and London dressmakers did not come cheap. Two such wardrobes were not to be paid for by the estate's income in one year. Honoria had accidentally seen the milliner's bill for her season and shuddered to think of it - her bonnets alone had been ruinously expensive. She had looked forward to her second season, where her wardrobe could be adapted at very little cost to give it a new look and Serena would also have her fill of new walking dresses and riding habits, bonnets and stockings. If she were in London with her sister, she might actually enjoy it.

'Poor Serena. What are her chances of a suitable match in this restricted neighbourhood?' Mama continued, 'And indeed, Honoria, if she does not like this match. Though how she could fail to like a charming, handsome man like Mr Allison is beyond me,' she finished.

'Do not forget rich,' teased her husband.

'When I think of the girls who tried to catch him all season! And then he came to us – specifically asked to be presented to her as a partner for the waltz, as dear Lady Carlisle informed me later - but she showed no triumph at all. And now, she will not give an opinion. She is strangely reticent about the subject.'

'Well, well, it is no doubt her shyness. She will be more relaxed when she sees Allison among the family.'

'So much rests upon it.' There was a pause. 'Dickie's commission?'

He laughed, but it sounded sour from her always cheerful Papa. 'Wilbert has promised to buy it from his next win at Faro.'

'Hah!' said Mama bitterly.

Honoria was free. She went towards the breakfast room rather noisily.

'Are there muffins?' she asked gaily.

'How on earth do you come to be engaged to *him*?'

Honoria was jolted back to the present by Serena's outcry. She gazed in dread over her sister's dark curls and saw a sober figure in a black coat and dull breaches, with a wide-brimmed, antediluvian hat walking towards the house. She gave an involuntary giggle.

'Oh, that is only Mr Scribster, his friend.'

'*He* you remember!' laughed Serena. 'Is he as dull as his hat?'

Honoria remembered Mr Scribster's long, miserable face, framed with two lank curtains of hair, at several parties. She thought it odd that a gentleman so patently uninterested in the events should bother to attend. And indeed her mother had whispered the same to her. Honoria must be present where her parents willed her - but surely a gentleman should be free not to? But Mr. Scribster attended in company with Lord Salcomb or Mr Allison with a face suitable for a wake.

'Yes,' said Honoria. 'He never looks happy to be anywhere. And generally converses with no one. Though occasionally I saw him speak to Mr Allison in his grave way and Mr. Allison *laughed.*'

'Maybe it's like when Sir Henry Horton comes to dinner.' Sir Henry was nicknamed among the children "The Harbinger of Gloom". 'Papa laughs so much at his doomsday declarations that he is the only man in the county that actually looks forward to him coming.'

Honoria spotted another man exiting the chaise, this one in biscuit coloured breaches above shiny white-topped Hessian boots. His travelling coat almost swept the ground, and Serena said, 'Well, he's more the thing at any rate. Pity we cannot see his face. You should be prepared. However, he *walks* like a handsome man.' She giggled, 'Or at all events, a rich one.'

The door behind them had opened. 'Serena, you will guard your tongue,' said their mama. Lady Fenton, also known as Lady Cynthia (as she was the daughter of a peer) was the pattern card from which her beautiful daughters were formed. A dark-haired, plump, but stylish matron who looked as good as one could, she said of herself, when one had borne seven bouncing babies. Now she smiled, though, and Honoria felt another bar in her cage. How could she dash her mother's hopes? 'Straighten your dresses, girls, and come downstairs.'

Benedict winked and walked off with his parent.

There were no looking glasses in their bedroom, so as not to foster vanity. But as they straightened the ribbons of the new dresses Mama had thought appropriate to the occasion, they acted as each other's glass and pulled at hair ribbons and curls as need be. The Misses Fenton looked as close to twins as sisters separated by two years could, dark curls and dark slanted eyes and lips that curled at the corners to give them the appearance of a smile even in repose. Their brother Benedict said they resembled a couple of cats, but then he would say that. Serena had told him to watch his tongue or they might scratch.

The children, Norman, Edward, Cedric and Angelica, were not to be admitted to the drawing room - but they bowled out of the nursery to watch the sisters descend the stairs in state. As Serena tripped on a cricket ball, she looked back and stuck her tongue out at the grinning eight-year-old Cedric. Edward, ten, cuffed his younger brother and threw him into the nursery by the scruff of his neck. The eldest, Norman, twelve, a beefy chap, lifted little three-year-old Angelica who showed a disposition to follow her sisters. On the matter of unruly behaviour today, Mama had them all warned.

As the stairs turned on the landing, the sisters realised there was no one in the large square hall to see their dignified descent, so Serena tripped down excitedly, whilst her sister made the slow march of a hearse follower. As Serena gestured her down, Honoria knew that her sister's excitement came from a lack of society in their neighbourhood. She herself had enjoyed a London season, whilst Serena had never been further than Harrogate. She was down at last and they walked to the door of the salon, where she shot her hand out to delay Serena. She took a breath and squared her shoulders. Oh well, this time she should at least

Beth and the Mistaken Identity

see what he looked like.

Two gentlemen stood by the fire with their backs to the door, conversing with Papa and Dickie. As the door opened, they turned and Honoria was focused on the square-shouldered gentleman, whose height rivalled Benedict's and quite dwarfed her sturdy papa. His face was nearly in view, Sir Ranalph was saying, 'These are my precious jewels!' The face was visible for only a moment before Serena gave a yelp of surprise and moved forward a pace. Honoria turned to her.

'But it's you!' Serena cried.

Everyone looked confused and a little shocked, not least Serena who grasped her hands in front of her and regarded the carpet. There seemed to be no doubt that she had addressed Mr Allison.

Honoria could see him now, the dimpled chin and strong jaw she remembered, and topped by a classical nose, deep set hazel eyes and the hairstyle of a Roman Emperor. Admirable, she supposed, but with a smile dying on his lips, he had turned from relaxed guest to stuffed animal, with only his eyes moving between one sister and another. His gaze fell, and he said the most peculiar thing.

'Blue slippers.'

GetBook.at/Honoria

Printed in Great Britain
by Amazon